A Cricket of a Girl

AC ESMAHAN

ISBN-13: 978-1541149014
ISBN-10: 1541149017

CreateSpace Independent Publishing Platform, North Charleston, SC.
Available on Amazon.com and other retail outlets. Also available on Kindle

There are many things that can only be seen through eyes that have cried.

-Archbishop Oscar Romero

Chapter 1

El Salvador, 1958

Sesi

I promised Figo that I would write this story, but I've always felt that stories which begin at the beginning can be a little, you know, boring. And sometimes it's hard to even know where the beginning really is. Take my story, for instance. Does it begin a long time ago, way back when the Mayan and Pilpil Indians ruled this land, before the tall, white Spaniards arrived and conquered Cuzcatlán? That's what my country, El Salvador, used to be called before they changed its name. It means "land of the precious things."

Or does it begin when I'm born to my mother in 1944, as she sweats all alone in the mosquito-filled cabin? My grandparents built that house and she lived there with my father until he found out that she was pregnant with my youngest brother and he remembered and forgot at the same time. He remembered that he needed to go get some cigarettes from the market, then forgot where his house was and never came back.

No, I would argue that neither of these beginnings will do because sometimes things don't look at all like they will turn into something interesting. I mean, it's the same way even with plants. If you were new to the country, like my friend *Doña* Laura, and you didn't know any better, how could you ever guess

1

that the tiny, brown furry sprigs that you saw on a huge tree by the side of the road would someday evolve into large juicy mangoes and fall onto tin roofs of houses with a *thonk*?

There, I've gone and done it again. I was talking about how to begin my story and now I've gone and introduced you to some of my friends and told you about mango trees before you even settled into the story. Figo used to tell me that people had to listen closely to follow me, and they could not be like sloths, hanging in the high trees, casually observing the story from a distance. So, dear reader, I hope you are not wanting to be like a sloth, but more like a quetzal, which is a quick little bird which stays on my shoulder as I give you my version of how things happened.

Because, you see, I want to give you an honest account of things, even the parts that are not very pretty and are hard to tell. So I'm going to start with Sara in the village of Lourdes. I was fourteen years old and having left home at twelve, I was making my way to San Salvador, the capital city, where I eventually wanted to live and make good money. But the way was slow and I had stopped to work at her father's house as her nanny for a few years. Sara was very sweet and I loved that little girl dearly.

I'm not saying that she was easy to handle—sometimes she was a real pest. Like on this day, when my story begins. I had been trying to find a way to make her eat, which was a daily challenge with this girl, and it was a task rendered even more difficult by the fact that I was hungry myself and running out of ideas.

"If you sit still like a good little girl and eat your rice and beans, I'll tell you a story," I said. I knew that she liked stories. Who doesn't, really? There are thousands, or maybe even millions of good stories out there, and I love hearing and telling them.

2

Sara looked up at me with hesitant eyes and pushed her lower lip out in a pout. "But, Sesi, you know that I don't like rice and beans. I hate rice and beans! I don't want to eat the same thing every day."

She was always like that—saying ridiculous things. I mean, who ever heard of not liking rice and beans? It's like saying you don't like the sky or the magnificent volcanoes towering on the horizon, or breathing. Rice and beans are good food. It's not debatable.

I focused on Sara, taking in her clean, crisp yellow dress with pleats down the front of her chest, and her shiny black patent leather shoes. Like I said, I really liked Sara, but there was no denying that sometimes that little girl could act churlish. She had everything I did not have, and she still wanted more.

I bit my lip in momentary frustration. It feels really good to bite my lip sometimes. It helps me to think. I also closed my eyes and reminded myself, once again, that it was my job to watch Sara and that I had to be careful not to let my frustration show or that would be the end of that job for me. This should not be too much to remember when you are fourteen years old, I know, but sometimes my thoughts were not so kind.

So I swallowed my first, more vitriolic thought and said instead, "Come now, Sara, at least you have food to eat. You don't have to fill your stomach with grasshoppers and worms!"

Imagine that you're there with me, my little quetzal, sitting on my shoulder, in that stiff little dining room, with that serious wooden table frowning at you and those mean chairs whose straight backs would carve painful marks into your back if you leaned against them for more than a minute or two. The walls of the room were a dark cream color and probably should have been repainted a few years ago, but the house was too sad for that to happen. Anyway, if you can see yourself there with me and Sara, then you understand the magic of stories.

3

Sara crinkled her nose at me and said, *"Ew!"* in that way that let me know that she was receptive and willing to cooperate if I just managed to nudge her a bit more in the right direction. "Yes, ma'am," I said. Then I noticed that Sara's pout had turned into an impish grin, and I felt my former resentment melting away. "What if you had a big plate of slimy worms and even some giant black beetles?" I said, getting into the story of the moment. I love doing that. "If it wasn't rice and beans there on the table, then who knows? You might have to eat bugs, or moth eggs or even bat toenails! So go on and eat your rice and beans now!" I commanded sternly, but without raising my voice.

You see, as happens in most stories, there was a witch living in Sara's house. Oh, not literally, of course, but very nearly so. I'm speaking of Sara's grandmother, who was really mean, especially to me. I knew that it would not be a good idea to have *Doña* Fabiola overhear me if I raised my voice to the child. Although Sara was half my age, I understood that this seven-year-old girl was going to have a very different life from mine. She had a home and her father had money. She was going to school and if she got into trouble, people would be there to help her. She would have opportunities to learn and travel and work that would never be available to me. But I didn't resent this, it just was the way things were, like rice and beans. We both understood this.

"But I don't like them," whined the child. "Why do I have to eat anyway? Why can't there be a pill that I could take instead? I don't like eating."

I clucked disapprovingly, pursing my lips. I do that a lot, especially when I'm upset. I looked off into the distance, out the window, and stared at the deep green leaves of the banana plants growing enthusiastically toward the back of the patio. Behind it, an enormous, scarlet bougainvillea, laden with flowers, crept up the white-washed wall, like a giant lizard, sticking its toes out at odd angles to hold on to the vertical surface.

It was so peaceful outside, with the deep azure sky and the warm, fragrant breeze. I did not want to be indoors, in that mean little house, trying to convince Sara to eat. I wanted to be out there, playing by the river, collecting mangoes for my mother, or talking to my brothers, but those were not options for me anymore. They would never again be options, now that I had left home.

My mother did not make me leave the home, I should point out. But it was clear that there simply was not enough money, what with my two younger brothers to feed, and my father still having forgotten all about us. It was clear that if I could get a job in another house, then those people would feed me and pay me and I could send some money back to my mother every month. So that's what I did. I worked at a couple of other houses, and now I was working at Sara's house.

"Sesi," she said, "why do we have to eat anyway?"

I registered her words in the back part of my mind, not the important part like the formal sitting room of a house, but rather the maids' quarters, where we stash people's words when other, more important thoughts are being courted. I was thinking of my mother and of how I was looking forward to seeing her again in two weeks, when I got some time off from this job.

"Sesi? Why are you looking outside? Sesi! Look at me!"

At her insistence, I tore my gaze from the window and stared down at the pleading child. Her plate was still almost untouched. I sighed and reached for her fork.

"Well, Sarita, maybe someday there will be a pill, but for now, there isn't one and this is what we have to eat. Here, let me help you. You're too big for this, you know? Seven-year-olds are supposed to feed themselves. But just this once, I'll help you. Your grandmother told me what the doctor said last week. Do

5

you remember what he said?"

The little girl nodded. "He said 'Sara, if you don't eat you will get skinnier and skinnier, and eventually you will get so skinny that you will be able to walk in through the crack between the door and the frame.' " As she spoke, Sara changed her voice to make it deeper, emulating the doctor, and I had to really concentrate not to laugh.

"Exactly," I said as I deftly heaped the rich brown, pasty beans onto the mound of white rice and then filled the fork and handed it to the child.

Sara accepted the utensil, eying it skeptically. "But, Sesi, that can't happen!" she protested as she nibbled a small bite of food from the tip of the fork.

That's the difference, you see? You can always tell a rich person from a poor person by the way they eat. You would never have caught me or my brothers or anyone in the small village where I come from nibbling from a fork. We would scarf the food down and be asking for more even if our tummies were taught and satiated. It's because we knew instinctively that food was a flighty, skittish companion and we never took it for granted. Nibbling was a luxury none of us had ever experienced.

"Oh, you never know. Maybe you'll get so skinny that when you go to a party, and you turn sideways, no one will even know that you are there and they won't speak to you and you'll have a terrible time. No one will want to dance with you or anything."

"Well, then I won't go to parties," Sara said, sticking out her lower lip. Again. She had really mastered the pouting act. She placed the fork, still more than half-filled with food, on the edge of her plate and crossed her arms. "I don't like rice and beans," she declared emphatically, as if I'd forgotten.

That's when I realized that I would have to use a

6

different tactic. I remembered how my mother had fed my brother when he was a baby and I said, "Here, let's make a *casamiento*. Watch."

I reached for Sara's fork again, tapped it against the edge of the plate to dislodge its contents, and then quickly mixed the rice and the lovely lumpy beans, which were the color of rich mahogany, until the rice was thoroughly trapped in the delicious mushy mass. Sara frowned at me, of course, but to her credit, she made no comment.

Then I grabbed the plastic container of salt, which was clumpy from the moist air, and removed the lid. By gently shaking, I coaxed a small mound of salt onto the side of the child's plate. It looked like a grainy, white volcano. Then I placed a small dollop of thick, rich Salvadoran cream, the best in the whole world, on top of the rice and bean mixture. Next, I grabbed the small glass decanter that held the olive oil, and poured a thin stream of the golden liquid over the cream. Finally, I took a small fork full of the rice and beans mixture with cream and oil and dipped it gingerly into the salt volcano. "Now, open wide," I said, using my 'no-nonsense' voice.

Whether it was that she was surprised by the culinary alterations she had witnessed, or that she was finally becoming hungry after stalling for so long, I couldn't tell, but whatever the case, Sara finally relented and complied.

"Better?"

She chewed thoughtfully for a moment before she conceded a small nod.

Encouraged, I repeated the process on a second forkful of *casamiento* and said, "Here, take the fork. Like I said, you're way too old for me to be feeding you! You eat and I'll tell you a story. Here, have a piece of tortilla with it too."

To kind of help her along I tore off a small corner of the

7

palm-sized, slightly toasted, cornmeal tortilla. A stack of fresh Salvadoran tortillas, thick and piping hot, were delivered daily to each household and their delicious smell, a smell I'd known since infancy, made my stomach grumble. Sara reached for the piece of tortilla and stuffed it in her mouth, nodding.

I swallowed saliva, ignoring the protestations of my stomach which seemed to have become as hollow as a brand-new piñata. I knew that the little girl would not consume all of the tortillas on the plate, but I was trying to behave so I resisted taking one for myself. It wasn't easy, I promise you, but I knew that it would be my turn to eat later, with the other maids in the kitchen, once the evil grandmother and her son-in-law had taken their dinner.

"Now, let me see, have I told you the one about the Monkey Princess?" I asked, as if puzzled and unsure.

Sara nodded. "But, tell me again! I like that story."

You see, this is one of the reasons I loved Sara so much. Who doesn't like someone who knows your stories but wants to hear them again anyway?

I reached for my mug of lukewarm tea and took a sip. At least that was allowed. Tea helped to calm the rumbling under my ribs. The mug from which I drank had become a left-handed one because there was an annoying chip on the rim which tore at my upper lip if I held the cup by the handle in my right hand.

A long dark crack ran like a lightning strike from the chip into the interior of the mug, and as I drank, I could see more and more of the jagged line. I liked looking at it and watching it grow longer with each sip I took.

Back then, when I worked in that house where Sara lived, I was only allowed to drink from this particular mug. Each of us *muchachas*, which are the people who work in houses, had one mug that was assigned to us and all of the other mugs were

8

for the use of the family, but this did not bother me. It was a far better life here in their home than any I had ever known. So I swallowed the tea, nodded at Sara to take another bite, and began my story.

"A long time ago, in the village of Sonsonate, on the side of a very high and quite ancient volcano, there lived a poor woman with her daughter." I had told this story dozens of times, not just to Sara, but to other children I had minded, and sometimes to the other *muchachas* who befriended me when I first left my mother's home and began working as a servant. Although the story was a very long one, it was also one of my favorites. Often the story would take days to finish, but I had found that my listeners relished its length as much as I did.

"And they lived by the river!" said Sara.

"Yes, now take another bite," I said, pausing long enough to see the next grudging forkful enter the child's mouth. Sara was not eager to comply, but I crossed my arms. This was partly to look more impressive, and partly to press my tummy so it wouldn't growl quite so loudly. Sara stared at me for a moment, her mouth beginning to curve into a pout again, but then she decided to give in. She took another bite and began chewing very slowly, the way I did sometimes when I knew that there was not much food and I needed it to last. We had the same behavior for two very different reasons.

I nodded approvingly—at least she was somewhat complying—and continued. "There was a small river, a creek, really, that was born high in the jungle on the side of the volcano on which they lived. This creek swelled every afternoon when the rains came and eventually it flowed, in hearty laughter, past their house. Their house was not a big one like this one. It was a small, plain house, made entirely of wood. The mother had built the house with the help of her two brothers many years before. The mother's two brothers had gone away, to get work in the big

9

city, San Salvador, and the mother had stayed there in her small hut, on the edge of the jungle, with her daughter, Mariángeles. They lived alone but they were not afraid. They made tortillas and every day Mariángeles would take them into the village to sell them, and then come back with the money at night. When her mother ran out of corn flour or salt, she would send her daughter into town and have her bring back some pretty heavy bags, which Mariángeles balanced on her head."

I wasn't making this part up. Back when I was a little girl, still living at home, I had often seen how women carried huge burdens, weighing twenty or twenty-five kilos, balanced on their heads as they went to and from the market. They would twist a towel tightly into the shape of a rope and then they would coil it on a flat surface to create a soft plate that they would place on the top of their heads. Then they would put the basket or ceramic pot on top of that and balance it there, sometimes reaching up with one hand to hold it steady as they walked. The good thing about this is that it makes you have really good posture.

Most often the heavy baskets contained rich tropical fruits: plantains, bananas, sugar cane, mangos, pineapples, guavas, *marañones*—these last ones are my favorite fruit because you can save the seeds and roast them later. They are called cashews and I understand that they can be quite expensive in other parts of the world. That's what *Doña* Laura told me— but I'm getting ahead of myself. I'll tell you more about her later.

Anyway, I had learned how to carry baskets atop my head like that too, to help my mother, though mine were never very big or heavy like those other women's were. Once, you're not going to believe this but it's true, a woman walked into the market carrying a wide basket of live chickens, perhaps fifteen or twenty of them, atop her head. That's not the unbelievable part—that happens all the time. But as she neared the stand where she would sell them, a little boy who was about three years old, riding on his father's shoulders, reached out as they passed the woman and grabbed one of the chickens, holding it fast by its neck. And you know how little kids are—at least I know my brother was this way—they grab something and hold it tightly and don't let go no matter what. So the little boy clutched that chicken by its neck until they got home.

The father later said that he did not realize that his son had the pullet, which the little boy had continued to grip mortally tight. Its poor head drooped lifelessly over his fist by the time they got home. When the son was lowered from his father's shoulders and they found his stolen chicken, it would have been nearly impossible to go back and find which vendor had been the victim of the unplanned theft, so they kept it and made chicken soup for dinner.

Now, I believe this story since I know the family that it happened to, but I can understand your skepticism. Sometimes people in El Salvador, especially people from small towns, can really stretch the truth. You are probably wondering how could someone carrying a child not feel the extra weight of the chicken or see the limp, feathery body out of the corner of his eye as he walked? I can't explain everything. All I can say is that sometimes, strange things happen.

Anyway, Sara looked up at me solemnly and nodded expectantly, her long, dark ponytails bobbing up and down over the front of her yellow dress. It reminded me of how much I loved the stories my aunt used to tell when I was little, so I carried on.

"Every morning, when she awoke, Mariángeles would go to the river to get buckets of water which they would use to make the tortillas and for washing up. On Sundays, she would stay on the riverbank for half an hour, washing her long, beautiful black hair in the chortling waters before bringing back the buckets. Her hair was so long and so thick, that she didn't dare wash it more often, as the water level in the river always dropped on the day she dunked her hair in it, owing to how much water her hair soaked up."

"I'm going to grow my hair like that one day too!" Sara chuckled, pulling at her hair now, as if to urge it to begin growing faster right away.

"Oh, in that case, you'll have to be sure you have plenty of water to wash your hair!" I said, reaching out to grasp one of her ponytails and inspect it. It was shiny and dark and still tied with the pretty ribbon I had used that morning. "Yes, I think you're right. It's so thick that people might not be able to get any water to drink on the days you wash your hair!"

That made her giggle gleefully.

"Time for another bite, Sarita. Okay, good. Shall I continue with the story? All right. One day, as Mariángeles was washing her hair in the river, an evil spirit came to her in the form of a monkey. He had an ugly, flat nose, big round ears and a long, furry tail. He looked at her, and he saw that she was very beautiful. Now, this evil spirit, he didn't have a wife and he really wanted one. So he asked Mariángeles to marry him. But when she saw him she realized that he was an evil spirit and she became very frightened. She refused him and shouting, she ran back home without even pausing to gather up the buckets.

"The monkey spirit became very angry with her for turning him down. He gnashed his yellow teeth and he snapped his hairy fingers and frantically shook his ugly tail. Then he sat down on a river rock to think of how he could punish her. Finally, he decided that if she would not have him in marriage, then she would have no one for a husband. Ever. He summoned his dark spirit powers and, focusing on her beautiful image, cast a nasty spell on her. When Mariángeles woke up the next morning, she had the face of a monkey!"

Sometimes I get so carried away by the stories I'm

telling that I forget what I'm supposed to be doing, but this time, since my tummy was still complaining, I didn't forget. When I paused, I looked down at her plate and I was encouraged to see that the story was having its effect, and Sara had nearly finished eating. Of course, seeing her plate just made my stomach protest loudly again. It really has a one-track mind, that stomach of mine. Sara was ready for another tortilla, so I lifted the cloth towel that had been covering the warm, moist stack.

Now, I know I probably shouldn't tell you this because you don't know me very well yet and it may make you think poorly of me for being weak, but I have promised to write a true account of things so I will tell you anyway. I'm not sure if you will understand, but the smell of the steaming, hot tortillas was unforgivingly alluring and tempting, and it had been a long time since my breakfast. So I removed a tortilla from the stack to give to Sara, but instead of giving her the whole tortilla, I tore it in half, handed part of it to the child, then took a bite of the other part.

Big mistake. No sooner had I placed the warm deliciousness in my mouth than I heard the dining room door slam against the wall. *Doña* Fabiola, the witchy grandmother I warned you about, entered the room.

"You, you monster. No wonder the child is so thin! You eat all her food!" she shouted at me in her shrill voice.

Sara and I were both jolted by the sudden presence standing in the doorway. Her hair was painfully black, except for a narrow white line at the roots which outlined her withered face. She had slicked her hair into a tight knot at the back of her head. Her nostrils flared and her thin, purplish lips were livid with the excitement of having caught her prey, which was me.

My heart thumped wildly because, of course, she was right—I had no excuse for taking that bite. I quickly swallowed the small piece of tortilla, which went down like sandpaper,

13

scratching my throat and getting stuck half way down. For a moment I was afraid I would need to cough.

"I ate the food, *abuelita*," said Sara. "Sesi made me a *casamiento* and I ate it all. See?"

Yes, she stood up for me. She was a real treasure, that little Sara, and you can see why I loved her. She held up her plate, still streaked with muddy lines from where her fork had scraped away at the beans.

Doña Fabiola did not look at it. She addressed Sara, but kept her bloodshot eyes fixed on me and said angrily, "Don't lie to me, Sara, I just saw that damn girl eating your food! Now, off with you to your room and I don't want to hear anything more from you! Go on, before I slap you!"

My eyes darted to Sara, who looked stricken. For a brief second her eyes locked with mine and she pleaded silently with me to say something, but I said nothing. What could I say? Instead I motioned by pointing with my lips, which I extended to look like a sideways kiss, for Sara to follow her grandmother's instructions, and then I lowered my gaze to the table and the floor while I silently gathered the plate and utensils to take them to be washed.

Sara began to protest again, but her grandmother raised her hand in a threatening gesture—I saw this out of the corner of my eye as it was such a brusque movement, and at that, the little girl turned and ran out of the room, her shiny black shoes tapping on the tiled floor as she fled.

"No dinner for you tonight, *muchacha*," said *Doña* Fabiola in the high, mean voice she reserved for me. I was not her favorite person in the household.

"You've obviously had enough. Are you trying to kill my granddaughter? Eating her food when you know she's too skinny? *Puta!*"

14

I didn't relish being called a bitch, but I knew better than to answer back. Once a cricket shows its hiding place, it can soon find itself on the underside of a shoe, the black juice of its guts leaking pathetically out. So I kept my mouth closed and my head down. I finished gathering the articles from Sara's dinner and scurried off to the safety of the kitchen.

But there was no safety in the kitchen either. "To your room, dammit," she hissed.

I turned and ran to my room and from there I heard her call sweetly to Sara's father that she would have his dinner out soon. It was incredible to me how she could be so two-faced.

Chapter 2

Sesi

"When her mother saw Mariángeles with her monkey face, she was very upset, of course, and she knew that their lives were changed forever. Her daughter could no longer go into the village to sell the tortillas because no one would buy them from her with a face like that, all covered with glossy, dark fur.

"So that morning her mother went into the village by herself. She sold all of the tortillas, but instead of taking the money home, as Mariángeles would have done, she went to the house of the woman who everyone said was a witch."

Before we go any farther, my little quetzal, let me explain something. *Doña* Laura told me that up in the United States people think that all witches are bad. You'll have noted that I've mentioned witches several times since I started telling you my story, so let me clarify: the one in this fairy tale was a nice, kind one, not like Sara's grandmother. Although, don't get me wrong, Sara's *abuela* was not rotten to the core either, as you'll see later.

Sara squeezed my hand and swung it a little more wildly than necessary as we walked. She frequently did that. It was the next morning, still early, and we were on our way to her school, which was almost a kilometer away. I always walked her to school because even though it was a small village, it would not have been safe for her to walk alone.

Now that I think of it, if anyone had wanted to do us harm, I don't think having me along would have protected Sara much at all. I'd like to think I would have been quick-witted, strong and resourceful, but I'm very glad I never had the opportunity to find out.

I remember that morning clearly though, not because anything special happened, but because it was a very typical day. At the time, I remember feeling that there would be many months and years filled with mornings like that. I would have years of walking to school with Sara, and telling her stories and feeling her swing my arm. But of course, I was wrong. Life would soon change drastically. Oh, there I go again, getting too far ahead of myself. Let me just say that now when I look back on that morning, it makes me feel good.

It was sunny and warm, but not unpleasantly so, and the sounds and smells of the village waking up greeted us as we walked along. Someone was pounding away with a hammer at a tiled wall that was being replaced in the store we had just passed. The sweet, ripe smell of mangoes being hawked on the sidewalks mingled with the pungent smell of urine from stray dogs that had relieved themselves on the wooden poles that held the dozens of electricity lines. And farther on, bicycles and a few cars, honking and belching out black exhaust fumes, competed for space on the narrow road as traffic steadily increased.

We walked hand-in-hand, and from behind, it probably looked as if I was not much older than Sara, although it would have been clear from my attire that I was the servant and not an older sister. Sara's stark white uniform with its blue leather belt and blue collar, a large circle whose edges sat on her shoulders, contrasted with my faded olive green dress. Likewise, Sara's shiny leather shoes and white socks trimmed in curly lace demarcated her status, as opposed to the dirty sandals that I wore

17

to protect my bare feet and which slapped against the sidewalk as if helping it clap out a melody with each step. However, I think it's safe to say that on that particular morning, both of us were oblivious to the contrasts as we shared the story of the Monkey Princess.

"The mother handed the witch her entire day's worth of tortilla money," I said, "and begged her to find a way to turn her daughter's face back to normal. The witch felt quite sorry for the mother, so she gave her a box of matches that she had found that morning down by the river. But, these were not ordinary matches that she had found."

"They're for Mariángeles! She needs to give them to her!" said Sara, now skipping with excitement, and swinging my entire arm up and down.

I could feel the palm of her hand becoming sweaty in mine, but I kept a firm grasp of her hand. Sara's school bag containing three bound notebooks, and three pencils whose sinuous black tips I had sharpened that morning with a paring knife, was slung over my right shoulder. We were about half way to her school.

"Yes, Sarita, you're very right! The old woman realized that the box of matches had magical powers for there were words written in an almost forgotten, ancient and secret language, on the side. To everyone else, the words just looked like little scratch marks, but the witch could decipher them. She held up the box and read the letters once more:

'For she whose hair grows dark and sleek,
covering brow and hiding cheek,
that she may use these matches well,
to rid herself of the simian spell.'

18

"Now, the old woman, who was a very wise and kind witch, had learned from her mother and her grandmother that these types of spells were perilous. She knew that this magic would bring great evil upon anyone who interfered with it, so she dared not keep the matches for herself even though she realized that they could do great magic. A long time ago, someone had interfered with the great magic, and she had been turned into a poisonous tree frog. So the old woman, who did not want to become an ugly old poisonous tree frog, carefully handed the box of three magic matches to Mariángeles' mother.

" 'You must give these to your daughter and tell her to use them only when the need is great. Each match will grant a wish when it is lit, but she must be very careful. Tell her that. Tell her that she must think about her wishes very well. Only she can make the wishes, and if she wishes for the wrong thing, she will have to keep her monkey face all her life,' the old witch assured her.

"The mother thanked the witch and returned home with the matches tucked in a tiny box, pressed into her bosom."

I sighed. I don't really know what it is, but when I get into the meat of a story, it's almost as if I am remembering it as if it really happened, rather than just telling it from my imagination. Have you ever felt that way? Have you ever imagined something so well that you feel it in your bones, beckoning you onward until it tells itself?

We were at a traffic light now, and while we waited for it to turn green, I looked up at the tangle of heavy, black electric wires that crisscrossed the intersection and threaded their way between poles. There were so many, more than thirty or forty lines, as if a giant black spider had gotten lazy and spun her black silk back and forth instead of going farther afield. And for just a second I was frightened, wondering what would happen to me if the spider caught us.

19

"More story!" Sara demanded, obviously noting my distraction with the wires.

I smiled at her fondly. I admired the spunk of this little girl who had already gone through so much in her life.

"The years passed, they adjusted their lives, and Mariángeles took on the cooking so her mother could go out to sell the tortillas every morning. Over time, Mariángeles became a very good cook, and as the village grew, people began coming to their house to buy the tortillas, *pupusas*, fried plantains and pineapple cakes that she cooked. Eventually her mother no longer needed to go out every day to sell her tortillas as they had many customers.

"They saved their money in a little tin can which her mother hid in a hole in the floor in her bedroom, way under the bed. She also put the magic matches in that can. Eventually they had enough money to build a veranda on the house and put out some small tables and chairs. After that, word spread about their delicious food, and people traveling between Ahuachapan and San Salvador began making it a point to stop there for lunch or dinner.

"Several times young men who were traveling asked if they could marry the young cook, who stayed in the back with a bonnet pulled low over her face, but if they were ever allowed to see her without her bonnet, they would run off, breaking their promise.

"It got so bad that Mariángeles' mother, who was becoming old now, kept a frying pan on a hook by the door to whack the scoundrels on the head if they got too insistent, rather than allowing them to see her daughter and make her feel worse with their rejections."

At this point in my story we arrived at her school, and as usual, Sara gave me a quick little hug before accepting her school bag and lunch pail. Then she extracted a promise from me

20

that the story would resume after her classes before she finally turned and trudged into the school yard to join the throng of white-uniformed girls.

I stared after her once she had left, feeling a bit jealous, I admit, and wishing that I could go to school too. When I was her age I loved school, but my mother only let me go until I turned twelve. After that it was too dangerous for young women in rural towns to attend school. Girls were kidnapped and raped, my mother told me. And it was true, but here I was, walking by myself and not really worried about my own safety.

Well, sometimes I worried. Like everyone else, I had heard the stories. Women were kidnapped and sold to the sex trade or made into slaves and kept under lock and key. These were dark, scary tales that made me open my eyes wide and cross the road when I saw groups of men just standing around. On the way home from dropping off Sara, and on the way to get her at the end of the day, I always walked with purpose, sticking to the larger, well-traveled roads, and did not tarry.

That morning, I returned along the same path, practicing reading all of the signs I passed on the way home. Most of the notices were about political figures whose large, black and white faces assured the general public that he would be the one to put an end to the war with Honduras and improve everyone's lives. He would also inform the readers that Communism was the Enemy and that he would make sure that all Communists were eliminated.

Sometimes the political posters also had little flags of the United States on them. This was to remind people that they were the good guys and that the USSR were the bad ones. If you were against Communism, then that meant that you were for the gringos. At least that's the way Figo explained it to me later. when he drew me maps on the back of *pupusa* wrappers and told me about countries like the US and the USSR, thousands of

21

miles away. But really, I couldn't see what was in it for either of those two countries—why did they care what our politics were? Neither of them shared borders with El Salvador so it's not like we would help or hurt them depending on our choice of government. Ah, but I'm getting ahead of myself again. Come on now, my little feathered friend, and let's get back to Lourdes.

On my way back to the house the streets were noisier and more crowded, and I increased the tempo of my sandals slapping on the cement. As I walked, I thought about what lay ahead for the morning. I still had to sweep the kitchen and dining room, wash and dry the dishes, and fill the pila, a large cement basin, for the morning washing of clothes.

At least Sara was an only child. In my previous house, I had to take care of several children who were forever getting into trouble. One of them was Jorge. He was the youngest boy, only four years old and he hated to drink milk. I remember the time when he took his full glass of milk and snuck out to the back courtyard where we *muchachas* worked. He crept up to the pila, which had just been filled with about fifty liters of fresh water for the morning washing, and dumped the glass of milk into the water. I was very distressed to find the polluted, opaque water and it took me a few hours to drain the pila, wash it out with soap and re-fill it. He was a terror, that little boy!

Of course, being so young, Jorge could not be disciplined for such behavior. I was only thirteen at the time, but I knew that to speak of his behavior with his mother would only have brought trouble for me. I knew exactly what her words would have been.

"And what were you doing that you didn't notice this child walking half-way across the house with a glass of milk in his hand? What if he had dropped it and cut himself on the glass shards? Aren't you supposed to be watching him? Isn't this what we pay you to do? If you're incapable of this one simple task, then I think we can let you go this very afternoon."

She had a bad temper like that, kind of like Sara's grandmother. Maybe having *muchachas* gives you a bad temper? I don't know, but I kept this secret, along with several others regarding Jorge's behavior. When I couldn't stand it anymore in that house, I left to find work elsewhere.

I was about halfway back to Sara's house now, and I could hear the hammering of the workers tearing out the tile in that store again. The insistent, jarring noise made me wish my hearing wasn't as good. That thought made me laugh as I remembered a time when the little devil child snuck up behind the older maid, Jimena, a stout, matronly type who was hard of hearing. It was just a few minutes before she had to leave the house to pick up Jorge's older sister at school. Jorge stood there and surreptitiously tied her apron strings together in multiple knots. I guess they dangled tantalizingly behind her back and he couldn't resist. When Jimena reached behind herself to untie her apron so she could don a fresh one before leaving the house, she was infuriated to find the long string of knots, looking like a snake that had swallowed a dozen mice in a row. "Jorge!" she said in hoarse whisper. She gritted her teeth and I could tell that she wanted to scream at him, but *muchachas* were not allowed to scream or we would lose our jobs immediately.

I remember how I giggled (far from where Jimena could see me, of course.) But shortly thereafter I noticed that little Jorge's pranks were increasingly focused on me. He splashed fiercely and flooded the bathroom when I bathed him, he threw his food onto the walls, especially when it involved tomato sauce. And he screamed when I told him for the twentieth time that no, he could not play with the drawer of knives. It really made me wonder if he would make it to adulthood! And then one time I caught him playing with matches and I realized that he was too much of a menace. It was then that I decided that I had to leave.

23

The following Sunday morning, when the family came home from church, I met them at the door. I said goodbye and took my small plastic bag, packed with everything I owned in the world, and walked to the next village to seek work there.

That was a bit of a hard time. I did not have any luck and was forced to live off the kindness of other poor strangers who shared their meager meals with me from time to time. That was real hunger, not like the tortilla incident of the other night when I was feeding Sara. My stomach is spoiled now that I eat twice or even three times a day, every day.

Fortunately, the mango trees were full of ripe fruit and I survived eating these and a few other tropical fruits until I finally got to the village of Lourdes and found the sign in the window at Sara's house.

"Sara's mother recently passed away, so they are in need of a *niñera*, if you are interested," the older housekeeper informed me when I knocked at the door. Stepping back and looking at me more closely she added, "Though you look like you could use a *niñera* yourself, such a short little thing you are."

This made me a little mad because I was plenty old enough to work as a *niñera* and take care of a child. "I am fourteen years old, and I have lots of experience," I said. It was not quite true: I would be fourteen in six weeks, and the most I had done was observe how others cared for children while I swept and scrubbed and tried to take care of Jorge, but I had learned to make boastful proclamations. Hunger is a very good teacher.

Now I had been at Sara's house for over a year and although my life was complicated by *Doña* Fabiola's fits of temper, and *Don* Enrique's nightly drunken spells, things in general were pretty good. (Oh, I think I may not have mentioned that *Don* Enrique is Sara's father. Sorry, I meant to say that earlier. Maybe I procrastinated mentioning his name because he's not a nice man. That's what my friend *Doña* Laura would have said. She loved trying to figure out why people did things.)

Anyway, here at Sara's house there were four *muchachas*—myself and three others. I shared a bedroom with Miranda, a nice girl who was about ten years older than me. She was taller than me too, like nearly every other adult, and her body was a lot prettier than mine because she was plump. I was a skinny cricket of a girl. And she had curly brown hair that she parted on the side and then pulled back in a long braid down her back.

I'm ashamed to admit that when I first met Miranda I found it difficult not to stare at the scars on her face. Eventually, after we had been friends for several months, she told me that they were from an accident when she was little. Her father had gathered *marañon* seeds, those lovely nuts which are also called cashews when they are freed from their acidic shells. The seeds need to be roasted before they are opened, and if you do not take proper precautions for drying them, they can explode. Miranda was only two years old when she wandered too near the open fire and the roasting nuts exploded. She was extremely fortunate not to have lost an eye.

Her grandmother cured her wounds using plant salves, mostly aloe, and she remembered only faint impressions of the trauma, but her scars were a constant reminder of what can go wrong when toddlers are not supervised adequately.

Her scars were almost artistic, (though if you thought of it that way, you would have to admit that the artist was a novice) and covered her right cheek more than her left one. But, they were one of those things that people got used to with time. I mostly focused on her kind eyes when she spoke to me. She was the cook, and I knew that eventually I would be too old to watch children and would need to learn the skill, so I often begged

25

Miranda to teach me.

It's funny, even then I had an inkling that cooking would save me, but I didn't know who would teach me the good stuff. That will come later.

"I'll show you how to make some things next week," Miranda regularly promised at the end of the day, lowering herself gingerly to sit on her thin cot. Her legs were always swollen at the end of the day from all the standing she did, whether it was for preparing the food or doing the washing, so getting onto the low bed took some effort.

All of us *muchachas* slept in cots, not real beds with mattresses like Sara and her family. It wasn't that I expected to sleep in a bed with a mattress. At home I had slept in a hammock and that was nice. But since I started working, I mostly slept in cots unless I was traveling between jobs, making my way to San Salvador, and then I mostly slept on the ground.

The cots were pretty regular as they come. They were made of a piece of dark green canvas stretched tautly over a wooden frame, and nailed into place. They were as wide as my arm is long, and about a head longer than I am tall. Mine was fine for me but Miranda had no room left over when she lay down on hers.

The wooden frame was rough and the legs of the bed were like porcupines, ready to give anyone who carelessly brushed against them a healthy dose of sharp splinters in the calf. We learned to avoid these even in our sleep.

We had no sheets, but that was no matter because the climate in my country was not inclement, in general, so there was no need to cover up at night. *Doña* Laura once told me that little pieces of ice fall from the sky in the place where she grew up. She says no one can sleep there without sheets and blankets during the cold season.

For the sake of honesty, let me say that I believe most of what *Doña* Laura told me, but I think she must have been making this part up because I've thought about it and there's no way that solid water could get up there into the clouds. And even if it did get up there as vapor, and then it froze (which is what she explained to me when I pressed her) it makes no sense because I learned that heat rises and the higher things get, the closer they get to the sun. So, a cloud that is higher up than we are and is closer to the sun, would melt. Either that or, if it really was made of ice, then the whole cloud would fall down at once because ice is heavier than air. So I really don't believe that it would break into little pieces and fall like salt from a shaker.

But I let *Doña* Laura think that I believed her because she is a lot like me and likes to tell stories and we all like to be believed when we are telling our stories, even if we know that they are from our imagination. And besides, she was very nice to me and I really did want to believe her.

But, back to Miranda and me in our shared bedroom. We slept in the same cotton dresses that we wore all day. Most of us *muchachas* had only two or three dresses. It was enough. All you had to do was to make sure that the day you wore one dress, you washed the other one so it could dry. Clothes dried quickly on the lines in the patio.

We would hang the clean dress on one of the nails on the wall of our bedroom so it was ready to go, and there was never a problem if we had to change quickly if we happened to get dirty. Because we were, every one of us, scrupulous about our appearance. None of us wanted to look dirty or unkempt, even in our tired and worn out dresses.

At night, with the chores of another day safely tucked away, Miranda and I would hold whispered discussions until we fell asleep. One evening Miranda told me that in the capital city, San Salvador, there were houses so grand that all of the maids

27

wore uniforms: crisp dark blue dresses that did not constantly need to be mended. Hearing this made me feel all the more certain that someday, somehow, I would get to San Salvador and make a life for myself there. I just didn't know how long that would take.

Chapter 3

Sesi

Sara giggled. It was dinner time and once again she and I were locked in a battle at the dining room table. This time I was smarter and drank a full glass of water before sitting down, to be sure that my hunger would not get the better of me while I coaxed Sara to finish her dinner. I had been working in this house for over a year so you would have thought that I would have learned this trick months ago, but somehow I seem to need to trip over the same stone several times before I remember to step around it.

I looked at Sara's plate and saw that there was still food left on it.

"Come on, Sara, you're almost done. You ate the chicken really well. How about taking a few bites of tomato?" I coaxed.

She stiffened and shook her head.

"Ah, you don't like it?" I asked, feigning surprise. I looked at the wedge of tomato gravely, then nodded and said in a conspiratorial whisper, "I think I know what's wrong. I think that it must be..." and here I slid my eyes to either side, as if I was afraid of being overheard by some magical person, "well...it must be that you're not eating it the way the Monkey Princess would have prepared it."

29

Sara's shoulders relaxed and she was suddenly interested. "How does she have it?" she asked, wide-eyed.

"With lemon and salt, of course. Does your tomato have that?"

Sara shook her head, and I did not miss the spark of curiosity in her eyes.

"Not eating it with lemon?" I said in an exaggeratedly shocked voice and shook my right hand vigorously, a few times, allowing my fingers to make a slapping sound against one another. It's a typical Salvadoran gesture that roughly translates to, "Oh, my goodness!" I later taught *Doña* Laura how to do this. It's a very common expression but I guess the people in America are too worried about chunks of clouds falling on them to use their hands to speak the way we do here.

"Well, then, we had better fix that right away," I said, rising and crossing to the bowl of fruit on the other end of the table. I removed a bright yellow lemon, rubbed it on the edge of my apron, and then cut a slice and removed the seeds with the tip of a notched knife. I squeezed the boat-shaped wedge generously over the tomato before reaching for Sara's fork, spearing a bright chunk of the fruit and touching it lightly to the small volcano of salt that I had erected on her plate.

Sara took the fork and examined the chunk of tomato with its supple seeds and bright red skin. She hesitated for much longer than one could reasonably expect, then gingerly took a dainty bite. As she chewed, a small smile emerged.

"Okay, I see you would have made the Monkey Princess happy. She always liked to see her customers eating, you know, though she had to watch through a peep hole in the kitchen door because she couldn't let any of them see her face. Shall I continue with the story?"

"*Si!*" she agreed, completely satisfied. No trace of our

30

previous struggle over her food marked her face.

"Okay, take another bite. Where was I?"

Now mind you, I had recounted the Monkey Princess story to her several times by now, but she loved the repetition. When I would ask her where we were in the story, Sara would sometimes skip forward or backward in the plot and have me pick up the tale at an entirely different part from where we had last left off.

At first I was taken aback and tried to remind Sara that no, we had actually stopped the narrative somewhere else. But soon she made it clear that she knew exactly what she was doing, skipping around like that. Since she knew the story so well, she would think of a scene that she most desired to hear about at that particular moment.

One day I told Miranda about this odd behavior and she said, "She's just like her father with his record player. He has his favorite records that he plays over and over again, and he'll stop in the middle, then come back and move the needle to an earlier or a later track, depending on his mood."

So after that I didn't worry about her grasshopper behavior, jumping back and forth, and I just chalked it up to her being her father's daughter.

We were at the part where the witch was handing over the magic matches, but I saw Sara making an exaggerated, pensive face and then suddenly brighten. "Bad men hurt her feelings so her mom had to hit them with frying pans!"

"Ah, yes!" said I laughing. It really did make telling the story more fun this way, I must admit. "You're very clever, aren't you? Okay, let me see here. Hmm, so different men wanted to meet Mariángeles and they always changed their minds as soon as they saw her monkey face. This went on for quite some time, and occasionally one of the men that came through the town and stopped at the restaurant would even claim that he was a prince or something, but in the end, they all left running if they ever got a chance to see her."

"And Mariángeles never used the magic matches to make any of them like her," Sara said solemnly.

"Right you are, young lady. Mariángeles' mother was shrewd and she had warned Mariángeles that using the matches that way would have been a foolish use of the magic. We can't ever force anyone to like us against their will, can we? All we can do is to be true to ourselves and be good people and if they don't notice us, then it is not meant to be."

Sara nodded gravely. It was a lesson that I was particularly keen on having her learn since she was having some trouble with some mean girls at the school.

"Anyway, one day a young, good-looking guy, you know, black hair, big brown eyes, chiseled nose..."

"Handsome mustache," added Sara.

"A mustache? Are you sure he had a mustache?" I asked. *Don* Enrique had a mustache, but I had never cared for them. Maybe that was because I didn't much like him, either.

"Yes!" squealed Sara, delighted to be changing the plot a little bit. "And a beard!"

"Oh, no! Not a beard!" I declared, shaking my head vigorously. I guess I've always had something against male facial hair.

"All right, no beard but yes mustache," she conceded.

"Okay, a handsome young man with a...mustache, came into the restaurant and as usual, he loved the food and wanted to meet the young cook. When the mother said "no', he became more and more insistent that he really needed to meet her. The mother repeated her well-rehearsed explanation that her daughter was not pretty to look at. The man relented and dropped the matter momentarily, but he asked if he could spend the night as he was traveling. The mother saw that a storm was coming in from the west, a bad one, blowing in from the ocean, and it was getting late in the day, so she said that he could stay in their small living room. Unfortunately, that was all the space they had because, she reminded him, this was a restaurant, not a lodging house.

"The prince, for he was indeed a prince, traveling incognito, accepted. That night, very late, when all the rooms were dark and most of the village slept, he was awakened by the sound of very soft but very beautiful music. He crept outside, for the storm had passed by now and it was no longer raining, and he followed the sound around the side of the small house, to the Monkey Princess's bedroom.

"There she sat, with her back to the open window, playing the guitar and singing a beautiful but very sad song. He couldn't see her face, but he saw her long, shiny hair, falling all the way down her back in dark, wavy tresses, and he fell in love. 'I will marry this young woman, I don't care if she's ugly, I can see that she's beautiful in the most important ways,' he said to himself when he returned to his sofa. So the next day he asked the mother for her daughter's hand in marriage, and of course, the mother refused."

"But he asked again and again," interjected Sara.

I paused for a moment and looked pointedly at the abandoned tomato wedge until Sara rolled her eyes and then pierced another small chunk and began chewing it with exaggerated care.

"Yes, he was persistent. He convinced the mother to let him stay on for many days, by paying her very handsomely and helping to do many tasks around the restaurant. At first the mother protested, of course, but the prince was so nice and so

33

helpful, fixing things, carrying large buckets of water up from the river and bringing home huge, heavy sacks of corn flour for more tortillas, that in the end, she let him stay. After a few days, he made himself a straw mattress which he used to sleep on at night. He would tuck it away behind the sofa in the daytime, and draw it out only when the sun was setting.

"Every night he listened to Mariángeles singing, and every few days he asked the mother again for her daughter's hand in marriage. But each time, of course, she refused. So, one night when he crept up to Mariángeles' window to listen to her music, he decided to call out to her. And how did he know her name?"

"He had learned her name from hearing her mother call to her occasionally during the day!"

"That's right! Mariángeles was not used to being called from her bedroom window, and although she always wore a bonnet in the kitchen so no one could accidentally see her, in her own room, late at night, she was not wearing a bonnet. She involuntarily turned when she heard her name, and at that moment, the young prince saw her face. It was a startlingly ugly face, to be sure, all full of hair, but her eyes, a beautiful shade of green, were still hers, and the prince was immediately aware that there was more to this story.

"Mariángeles lifted her hands to her cheeks and turned away from him, but he did not run away as all the other men had done. Instead, he gently called her to the window sill where he talked to her, and the more they spoke, the more he loved her and the more she loved him.

"They met that way for many more nights, at the end of which he declared his love to her and she accepted him. The next morning, he called to Mariángeles from the main room, and she emerged from the kitchen, and took off her bonnet, even though it was daylight, and went to him. When Mariángeles' mother saw that the young man did not flinch or run away, and that her daughter also seemed happy, she relented and the two were soon married."

"But Mariángeles didn't want to move away!"

"No, she didn't."

"Because her mother was still alive," said Sara bravely.

My throat tightened when I heard her declaration. You see, part of the reason I loved Sara so much was that even though she led a life of privilege, a life I did not think I could ever have, I also knew that she had suffered a great deal. She was wounded deeply and in a way that I was not, since I still had a mother. But I didn't want to make her cry by speaking about it so I carried on with my story.

"Right. So they built an extension to the house and settled down to live right next door, and the prince helped in the day-to-day running of the restaurant, which now was a growing business. But he did not tell Mariángeles or her mother that he was a prince."

"But they found out when the messengers came!"

"Yes, now take another bite, there's a good girl. Yes, Sara, they found out. You see, only the oldest son could inherit the wealth and property of his father, and this prince, whose name was...what was his name?"

I stopped and waited for Sara's answer. I liked stopping as each time I could also motion toward her plate, and while her mind was occupied, Sara automatically took another bite. It had been a rather large tomato wedge, and it was nearly finished now.

"Um, let's say José," said Sara.

"José? Wasn't it a different name last time?"

"I want 'José' this time!"

35

"Fine, Prince José. Are you sure?"

Sara put down her fork and placed her hands on her hips in indignation so I continued, pretending to be repentant. "Okay, fine. So this José, Prince José with a moustache, was not the oldest son, nor was he the second oldest son, but, rather, he was the third and youngest son. So, he knew there wasn't much of a chance of ever inheriting the kingdom, which is why he had never said anything to Mariángeles or to her mother about his title.

"But, it seems that his father, the king, was not one to do things traditionally, and so instead of assuming that the oldest would get the kingdom, the old man had decided that he would visit with his three sons, get to know their new wives, for all three had been married in the last year, and then make his decision as to who would inherit what. So, on that day, about a year after Mariángeles and Ramón—"

"José!" Sara exclaimed, some exasperation creeping into her voice. She crossed her arms to make her point.

"Ah, yes," I said, winking. "Just checking to see if you were paying attention! So, a year after Mariángeles and José were married, the king's messengers arrived at the front door of their little house/restaurant and informed José that there was to be a ball at the castle, and that he and his wife were to travel there. The one request the king made was that each prince needed to bring a small cow for the milk."

"Because the king liked very, very fresh milk at breakfast!"

"Yes, it was a bit odd, I will admit. But anyway, suddenly José had a lot of explaining to do. But his wife and his mother-in-law listened well, and they were not angry that he had not told them before about being a prince. Instead, they busied themselves making plans for the trip. José did not have a fancy carriage in which to arrive, and this worried him very much, so that night Mariángeles drew out one of her three precious matches from the tin can under the floor board where it had been stored for years. She lit it carefully and then concentrated as she wished for a nice carriage.

"The next morning, parked behind the house, was a beautiful carriage with four large, prancing horses. The driver apologized profusely for having taken so long to get there, saying that he had gotten lost in the jungle, and he insisted that it would be his pleasure to escort them to the palace as soon as they were ready. They invited the mother to come too, but she said she preferred to stay and run the restaurant. So off went Mariángeles with José.

"On the trip, Mariángeles wore a bonnet with a small, dark veil that covered her face and José came up with the idea that they would say that she had really bad scars from a measles infection and was too shy to show her face. So they traveled, and in a few hours, they arrived at Acajutla, where the king's castle sat on a high cliff, overlooking the ocean.

"When their carriage pulled up to the large front doors of the castle, they were personally received by the king himself, and although the king said nothing, he was not impressed by the wives of the two older sons, who were rude and snobby as they stepped out of their carriages, each of which, by the way, was also larger and grander than José's. The gentle and unassuming wife of the king's youngest son pleased him the most.

"The next morning the king asked that the dairy cow of the eldest son be brought to the morning breakfast table. The son had found the largest cow, and it was so big that it would not fit through the door to get into the dining hall! It could not even fit through the doorway of the castle, so broad were its horns. After trying for almost an hour to get it through the door, turning its head from one side to the other, the staff had to lead it far afield and carry the milk in, which became cold and flavorless along the way!"

Sara giggled as she always did when this part of the story was told. She had finished eating now and it was time for her bath. I quickly cleared the plate and then led Sara by the hand. I wanted to keep her focused on the story so that she wouldn't even think of putting up a fuss about the bath.

"So then they brought in the second cow because the king really, really wanted fresh, warm milk!" Sara exclaimed, undressing herself to step into her bath. The house was modern and had running water, but it did not have hot water. Fortunately, Miranda had already heated water and filled the tub for her. I made a mental note to thank her later.

"Yes, they called for the second son to bring in his cow, which was much smaller. She entered through the castle doorway easily and passed right into the dining room, but when she got there, she refused to be milked. She fussed and fidgeted, and when any of the milk maids got close to her, she kicked until she knocked over the beautiful breakfast table, upsetting all of the fine silver and dishes. So she had to be removed and a very vexed and hungry king called for the third cow."

Sara was laughing heartily now. "But they didn't have one!"

"Right," I said. "Now, close your eyes, Sara, here comes the water to rinse your hair. There. So what did Mariángeles do?"

"She spent another match!" said Sara, holding her hands out blindly for a towel to dry her face.

I handed her a small towel and then continued with my story as I washed her back.

"Yes, poor thing, she used her second magic match. She lit it carefully and wished for a small dairy cow, and soon she found it, next to her carriage. It was a very petite cow, only as big as a goat."

"And it was gentle and docile," she said.

"Right you are, Sarita. Do you want to tell the rest of the story?"

She shook her head.

"All right. So Mariángeles led the little cow into the breakfast room of the castle and it stood patiently on a low table and gave fresh milk for all who wanted it. The king enjoyed his breakfast feast and was very happy with his youngest son. That night, there was to be the ball, and after the dinner and dancing, the king would announce his heir. This was when Mariángeles realized that she would have to use her last match."

"Not to get pretty."

"No, not to get pretty. You know the whole story, are you sure you still want to hear the rest?" I asked as I wrapped Sara in a large towel and rubbed her dry.

"Hear the rest. Hear the rest!" she chanted jovially, extracting her arms to clap along. I was beginning to fear that she might not be ready to go to sleep with all that energy.

I cocked my head at her as if I was trying to decide whether or not to continue. "Well, all right. Since you're almost finished, and you ate all of your dinner, I'll finish the story. What Mariángeles wished for was a beautiful, emerald green gown. And when she went up to her chamber, there it was, laid out on the bed, with a matching veil. 'I hope you will find that it is fitting, dear Lady,' said the servant.

"That night Mariángeles fixed her long dark hair in an elegant style, put on the lovely green gown and the silky green veil over her face. She met her husband at the bottom of the stairs and he proudly escorted her to dinner. At the table, the king placed Mariángeles in the chair right next to him and spoke with her and José.

39

"He heard from his youngest son about how happy they were, and what a wonderful person his wife was, kind, talented and intelligent. The king asked to see her face, but she said she was embarrassed, so he did not insist. As they ate, the other two wives, who were jealous of the attention Mariángeles was getting from the king, watched her carefully. This is how they noticed that every now and then she would put bits of rice and meat into the bosom of her dress."

I reached down and pulled out the front part of my dress, which was much flatter than how I imagined the dress of my princess would have been, and mimed placing small pieces of food into my bosom.

"The wives did not know why she did this, but they decided to do the same, just in case. When they all got up to dance after dinner ended, as Mariángeles whirled around, rose petals fell from the hem of her gown, and the ladies realized the bits of rice must have magically turned into flowers. So they danced too and twirled around too, but their rice and meat came out just as it had gone in..."

"And a big pack of stray dogs came onto the dance floor to eat up all the food and the king got really mad!" Sara practically screamed before dissolving into giggles.

I chuckled. Sara was now in her nightgown and so I led her to her bedroom.

"And then the king started choking!" she said, forcing a series of weak coughs.

"What happened next?" I asked, pulling back the sheets.

"The king turned red and then blue and stopped coughing because he couldn't breathe. And everyone was scared because that is how his wife had died when José was little. Now you."

"You're doing fine, go on," I said.

"No, you!"

"All right. Mariángeles grabbed him from behind and gave him a big hug, putting her fist in his tummy, and that made him spit out the chicken bone that he was choking on. Soon he was coughing again and his color returned."

"And then?" demanded Sara.

"Well, then Mariángeles took off her veil and everyone saw her, but not as a Monkey Princess anymore. She had been transformed into a beautiful young lady. She had her own face back. The curse had been broken when she used all three matches to wish for other things and not to change her own appearance. If she had used any of the matches to make her face pretty..."

"She would have been cursed to be ugly all her life because the evil spirit thought she was vain and selfish and he thought she really was going to use one of the wishes to be pretty again but he didn't know that she was smart and figured out not to do that!"

"Right again. And now, young lady, it's very late. Time to go to sleep."

"Sesi, did my mother die from choking?"

I took her hand and held it. "No, my sweetheart, your mother died from cancer."

She stared down at her blanket. For a moment I thought she would ask more questions, but instead she said, "A song!"

I rolled my eyes and shook my head—I had been right to suspect she would not go to bed that easily that night. "All right, just one," I said and then I sang in a very soft voice:

RIN, RIN, RIN, el grillo canta asi (The cricket sings like this,)

41

RIN, RIN, RIN, en la oscuridad. (when it is dark outside.)

¡Que grillito tan chillón! ¿A ver adonde está? (What a noisy little cricket! I wonder where it is?)

Tal vez en un rincón, chilla, chilla más y más. (Perhaps in some nook, chirping more and more.)

This little song had always struck me as a very appropriate one for the evening as the crickets increased the volume of their nocturnal calls.

When I finished my whispered song, I tucked the little girl in, helped her to say her prayers, shut off the light and left the room.

I have such fond memories of caring for Sara, but for some reason, that one and the morning that I walked her to school, the one I told you about earlier, those are the ones that stand out in my mind now. I wish I could have continued to stay on as her nanny for many years, watching her grow into a young woman, but that was not to be. Even at fourteen I had already learned that our hearts have longings for things which cannot be. I had wanted to stay home and go to school, and that could not be. Now I wanted to stay on and take care of Sara, but soon, that dream would also become ruined, like a stray dog that lingers in the road and then gets hit by a car. It happens all the time. I just wasn't used to it yet.

Chapter 4

Illinois, 1958

Laura

"Have you brought in the eggs yet, Laura?" her mother asked. It was a rhetorical question—if she had brought them in, they would be in the basket by the refrigerator, and they clearly were not. "Didn't I say that I wanted them in here this afternoon?"

"Yes, Mama. I'm really sorry. I was with cousin Jimmy. He was showing me the dog he shot. It was another one of those curs that was chasing the cows last Saturday."

"Lord ha' Mercy! Does he think there are any more out there?"

"He said there might be one more left. Or it might be a coyote. Hard to tell in the dark."

"Well, good thing he's getting them. But it's already dark outside and the chickens will be settling down for the night. Now hurry up and go out there and get those damn eggs or you'll not be eating any dinner tonight!"

Laura clenched her teeth and sullenly got to her feet. She trudged to the door where she stooped to pull on her mud boots. She was sixteen years old and if there was one thing she hated, it was collecting eggs in the chicken coop.

43

"And be quiet when you come back in," said her mother. "I've got a headache and I'm going to go to lie down for a spell now."

Laura grabbed the egg basket and went out the back door, dreading the chore as she did every day. Later on in life she would tell her friend Adel, "I'll never understand people who romanticize the life on a farm, putting pictures of chickens and cows on dishtowels and making little figurines of them. Clearly those people are city folk. Chickens and cows are nasty and no country person would want to have pictures of them around."

But on this particular night, Laura was not thinking those unkind thoughts about farm animals. She was instead thinking about school, and about what she wanted to do with her life. Encouraged by her English teacher, whom she adored, Laura had made a decision: she wanted to go to college, and she wanted to become a teacher. She only had two years left in high school, and it was time to make plans, her teacher had said. But it was 1958, and it was not a common thing for women to be educated. Especially women growing up on farms in the Midwest.

She knew without a doubt that her parents would oppose her plan. Her older brothers, both of whom had already left home, had the choice of higher education, but what use was all that learning for a woman, her mother had said. Women were better off not cluttering up their brains with strange ideas that would only cause trouble down the line.

Laura took a flashlight and headed out to the coop, unrolling the sleeves on her shirt and buttoning them at the cuffs as she walked. Her arms always had little scabs where the nasty hens pecked her as she tried to take their eggs. She hoped that perhaps, since it was later in the day than when she normally stole their eggs, they might be too drowsy to fight her.

A cock sporting dark, glossy feathers strode importantly in front of her as she neared the coop. With each step, he seemed

44

to lunge with his head and chest before carefully raising each talon high and then stepping daintily forward. It was almost as if he were leading the way to his private harem. Just as she reached the entrance, however, he squawked and headed in a different direction.

She pushed the door to the coop open and was immediately greeted with the heat and stench. Her sister swore that the henhouse did not have a smell, but to Laura, it definitely did. She began breathing through her mouth and concentrated on the task: the sooner she finished, the sooner she could exit the fetid coop. She shooed one hen away from her nest and raised the flashlight to inspect the place where it had been. No egg. She grumbled and moved on to the next one. This one held its ground more ardently, usually a good sign that it had something to protect, but again, no egg. She clenched her jaws and continued down the row.

The third and fourth hens had eggs that she took, but just as she withdrew an egg from the fifth nest, the hen turned back and pecked sharply at her arm. She pulled it quickly back and as she did so, the egg slipped from her grasp and fell to its demise. She cursed herself for her clumsiness, and in her anger, accidently inhaled a nose-full of the disgusting stench. She quickly returned to breathing through her mouth, and placed a handful of straw over the crushed egg. On her way out she would scoop it up and take it to the hogs as a treat.

After gathering a total of eight eggs, which she placed in the basket that she held over her left forearm, she gingerly picked up the cracked egg with some more straw and headed toward the sty. It felt good to be out in the fresh air again, and she took big gulps to clean out her airway. Even though the sun had finished setting, it was not as dark outside as it had been inside the chicken coop. She resumed breathing normally and picked her way between the clumps of grass and mud puddles.

The pigs greeted her warmly. They were dirty animals, to be sure, but they weren't nasty in the way that chickens were. Laura hated living on the farm, but most particularly she hated the chickens. She fed the pig who came closest—was it Spotty or Turnbull? It was hard to tell in the low light. Then she picked up her basket and headed back toward the farmhouse. She was looking down, making sure she would not trip on an errant furrow made by the large tractor wheels, and that's why she didn't see the shadow that lurked near the shed until she was upon it.

"Careful there, wouldn't want your mother to be pissed off at you for breaking any more eggs, now would you?" said the gravelly voice that she had learned to fear and hate. For years now, her father had been molesting her.

When she was younger, five years old, it had been more benign. He would enter the bathroom when she and her sister were taking a bath and after using the toilet to take a piss, he would reach into the bath water to rise off his private part, which he would hold at the level of their faces. Laura's younger sister, Sally, who was three years old, had even been curious once and reached up to touch it before Laura had quickly brushed her hand away. Their father had laughed heartily.

"It's all right. Let her feel how hard it is."

Other times, in broad daylight, he would emerge from the bushes, having relieved himself there instead of going into the house, and "accidentally" forget to tuck himself back into his pants as he made a point to walk by Laura when she was sitting by the barn, shucking corn. He only did this when he knew that his sons were out in the field and his wife was busy making supper.

"Oops!" he'd say and grin as he fumbled sloppily to button his pants over his bulging penis.

As she got older, around the time she turned nine, he

46

began cornering Laura at odd times, and asking her to feel his member. "It seems awfully hard and hot," he would say. "Do you think there's something wrong with it? Here, feel it and tell me what you think."

"No!" she would hiss and try to turn away. Sometimes she even managed to escape. But often he already had her in his vice-like grip and he would yank her hand toward him. If she made a fist, he would squeeze her arm so hard that she had bruises for days.

When she turned twelve, her father began "accidentally" touching her. He would pass her in the hallway and reach out and catch her ass as he stepped by, as if he needed to do that to keep his balance. Or he would insist that there was something on her chest that he had to wipe off, and then he would fondle her and make some remark about her 'ripe little peaches.'

Always there was the understood secrecy of these interactions. Laura felt ashamed and guilty, but he was bigger and stronger and when she tried to run away, he always managed to catch her. He was a big bully, stronger and faster that she was, and she did not know what she could do to stop his advances.

Her mother was distant at best, aggressively neglectful at worst. Laura knew that she would never have believed her allegations. She would probably have even accused Laura of bringing on his attentions. And Laura could not imagine telling one of her aunts or her teachers about what her father was doing—just the thought of speaking about his intrusions made her burn with shame. She was completely convinced that it was her fault for attracting his attention, her fault for somehow inciting him.

Laura worried constantly about what to do, and as she watched the animals wrestle with one another, whether it was the young cocks trying to establish supremacy, or the bucks of larger animals jousting and occasionally injuring each other, she slowly realized that one way to put a stop to her father would be to confront him. But first she would have to make sure that she would be stronger than him.

The opportunity to tip the scale had occurred when her cousin Jimmy asked her if she wanted to go hunting for rabbits. Suddenly it clicked in her mind—she did not have to be bigger or stronger than her father if she had a gun. She readily agreed and began to school herself in the use of a shotgun. That was a month ago.

Now, here was her father, cornering her in the dark, and she was utterly alone. The farmhouse was more than fifty feet away, and all the windows were closed. And if she made a run for it, he would probably catch her before she got very far. Unless she could make it to the cornfield and hide among the stalks. But that was unlikely too.

"Leave me alone," she said, taking a step backward and placing a protective hand over her basket to steady it.

"Now, now," he said, in a soft voice, "you shouldn't be scared of your old Pop. All I want is a little kiss. Can't a Pop ask his favorite daughter for a little kiss?"

Laura took another step backwards, desperately calculating the distance to the cornfield. If she darted quickly enough to the right, she might be able to make it. She kept her eyes on her father, watching to see which way he was going to lean. She was still edging away from him when suddenly she felt her ankle twist on clump of grass. She fell backwards and he was on her in an instant, his warm moist muzzle hissing into her ear that she had to keep her voice down or she would regret it.

She struggled with him, smelling the acridness of the cheap liquor he had been drinking. He put his large, grizzly mouth over hers and poked with his tongue inside as Laura twisted and squirmed helplessly under him.

"Stop! Stop it, Pop, I mean it," she said, in a voice that came out stronger and louder than any she had ever used before with him. "I know how to use a shotgun. Jimmy taught me and I got me one. I've got it hidden safe and so help me God I'll put a hole in you while you're sleeping if you don't get off me right now."

She felt his body suddenly go slack. Without waiting for him to change his mind she shoved him hard and scrambled away, running as fast as she could. She ran into the cornfield and then hunkered down, quietly hidden. He tried to follow her, but his gait was clumsy and, drunk as he was, he knew not to yell. He did not want to attract his wife's attention.

Laura waited for almost an hour until she was sure that he was either passed out or had stumbled off. Then she quietly made her way back to the farmhouse.

The next morning at breakfast her mother began the questioning. Everyone was having their morning oatmeal porridge. Her father was clean-shaven, though his nose was red and she could see scratch marks on his arms.

"What happened to you?" her mother asked her father, pointing to his arm.

He casually glanced at his arm and then said, "Those damn wild rose bushes. Got a bunch of them growing out by the far field. Got to clear them out."

"I'll help you, Pop," said Laura's younger brother, Steven.

"No you won't," said her mother. "Those are some very large thorns to make scratches that wide. Best you let your father handle them alone."

"But—" began Steven.

"Hush now!" said her mother dismissively and turned to Laura. "And you, shameful girl! All of those eggs were ruined!

Your father found the basket this morning when he went out to milk the cows. I have a mind to whip you for that."

She was prepared for this question. She had spent the whole time in the cornfield as well as part of the night trying to think of what she'd say to her mother.

"I'm awfully sorry, ma'am. I would have told you last night, but I didn't on account of your headache. It was a coyote that came at me, probably the same one that Jimmy saw over on their farm. It scared me so I dropped the basket and ran away. But don't you worry, it won't happen again. I've got a shotgun and I'm going to have it with me from now on, every time I go outside. If he ever sneaks up on me that way again, I'm going to shoot him between the eyes."

Her father made a choking noise and dropped his spoon.

"Did it go down the wrong way?" asked her mother, turning to look at him.

He nodded as he got up, still coughing and left the table.

"Well, just be careful you don't scare the cows when you shoot, you hear me?" said her mother, turning back to Laura. "All I need is to have them getting scared and drying up. Lord ha' Mercy!"

And so it was. Laura made sure to always take her shotgun with her, wherever she went on the farm, and especially if she went out once the sun was setting. She also went hunting with her cousin Jimmy as often as she could and bragged shamelessly about her uncanny aim when the family was sitting around the table at dinner.

On the evenings when her mother went to bed early, Laura made a point of cleaning her shotgun in the living room when her father was sitting there having a smoke on his pipe. She would rub the barrel till it shone and then point it at him, as if she were sighting him in the crosshairs. He would pretend not to notice, but he never touched her or Sally again.

Still, even without his abuse, life on the farm was hard. Her days began before dawn, helping to make breakfast or occasionally milk the cows before school started if her father's back was acting up. After school, she also spent time in the hot sun, weeding between the rows of tomatoes, beans or potatoes. In the winter, there were clothes to mend, food to be cooked and laundry to be ironed. The work never ended.

She studied hard and dreamed of moving far, far away from Illinois, someday, somehow.

Chapter 5

El Salvador, 1959

Sesi

After working in that sad house for a year and a half, I had observed that occasionally *Doña* Fabiola had good days. On these days, she would take Sara out to walk in the gardens of the park or she would sit down with Miranda and plan fabulous dinners for the week. Miranda told me that before Sara's mother died, *Doña* Fabiola was not a difficult person to get along with. She had her whims, of course, but in general, she was a reasonable member of the household.

But after she lost her daughter and more time passed, these good days became fewer and the bad ones piled up high, like the lemons in the fruit basket in December. One evening, having been in a foul mood all day, she found me in the kitchen, having dinner after I had put Sara to bed. I knew that she was going to pick a fight the moment she slammed the swinging doors of the kitchen back against the wall. I don't know what had set her off, but she stormed in, yelling at me for being a greedy pig and accusing me of indulging in dinner twice that day.

This was so ridiculously untrue that I kept my head down and my mouth shut as she leveled myriad accusations at me. I thought that not engaging her would calm her down sooner, but instead it seemed to enrage the old woman even further. She stepped closer to me as her tirade continued, until she was standing right over me, like a giant venomous spider hovering over a cricket.

In the background, I heard the front door push open and *Don* Enrique walked into the house. *Doña* Fabiola paused for a moment too, listening, and we heard him trip against the small entry table, which meant that he was drunk. Then she turned back to me and raised her arm up. I was afraid she would hit me, but the table where I was sitting was in the corner so I had nowhere to go. I hunched my shoulders and brought my arms in, protectively, ready to cover my head and make a dash for it if I saw a fist coming. She had never hit me before, but with some people, it's just a matter of starting and then they quickly get used to it and it's no big deal for them to do it over and over.

I know because I've seen how it is at the different places I've worked. Usually it's the men that hit, but believe me, the women can do so as well. I knew I'd leave immediately if anyone laid a hand on me, but I really preferred not to have to leave with a missing tooth or a black eye, if at all possible. Besides the obvious agony, you really can't apply for another job until you're healed and looking healthy again because otherwise the only place that would take you is another place that would add to your collection of bruises.

Then we heard *Don* Enrique enter the dining room. At that moment *Doña* Fabiola picked up my plate and emptied it into the trash. "No more for you, you insolent little pig!" she said in a quiet, venomous voice and immediately banished me to my room. I was glad to be out of that kitchen with no marks and I fled as fast as I could. As I sat on the cot breathing heavily for a few minutes, I heard *Don* Enrique holler that he was hungry. I wondered idly if that meant that I should take him a plate of food, but I figured that *Doña* Fabiola was probably still in the kitchen and would be very angry if I returned. I waited and soon heard her grunt that she was fixing him a plate. I sat listening quietly, my indignant stomach protesting its bad fortune. I'm telling you, it was quite spoiled.

After half an hour of sitting by myself in the cramped cement-floored bedroom, biting my lip for the sheer perverse pleasure of it, Miranda came into the room. I don't know how she did it, but somehow she had found a way to smuggle some food in for me. As I hungrily stuffed my mouth with bits of tortilla wrapped around a small mound of heavenly rice and beans, I suddenly remembered my manners.

"Thanks, Miranda, you're a true friend," I said, and I meant it.

"Honestly, I just don't understand why you didn't tell her that it was your first dinner? What would have been the harm in letting her know the truth? You hadn't done anything wrong."

I looked at Miranda and my eyes traveled briefly across the terrain of the scars on her face before they met her eyes. Then I shrugged my shoulders and said, "I don't think it would have made any difference."

Miranda chewed on this statement, working her jaw up and down distractedly. Like most people our age, she was already missing several large teeth and this made her need to chew things, even words, for hours at a time.

While I ate she sat on her cot and got busy sewing a hole that had developed in the skirt of her dress. "You're probably right," she said after several moments. "She seems to get fixated on people and picks on them a lot. You're the one she's obsessed with now."

I shrugged again and continued eating quickly. I remember being worried that *Doña* Fabiola would enter our bedroom—no place was off-limits to her—and find me there eating. I could imagine her rage. She would scream and shout and, worst of all, she would take away my food again. Miranda was a larger woman, and I knew that missing a meal probably wouldn't affect her as much.

"She wasn't always like this, you know, *Doña* Fabiola. She used to never drink..." said Miranda, her voice quite low. Outside the crickets were chirping loudly, conspiratorially drowning out our conversation from any potential eavesdroppers.

I nodded as I watched the deft, swift movements of her needle making its way across the fabric. Miranda was a really talented seamstress.

"But she's definitely getting worse. It must be the grief that is doing that to her. I know that I sure wouldn't trade places with her, no matter how much extra money that would mean," said Miranda without taking her eyes off her work.

I swallowed and contemplated her words.

"Death respects the rich more than the poor, but eventually it comes for everyone," said Miranda sagely. "And sometimes it gets confused and comes early. I used to be jealous of her, of the family, you know, before Sara's mom died. But now, living here with her good-for-nothing son-in-law and skinny little Sara, well, *Doña* Fabiola's life is not so great any more. She rarely ever goes out, and practically no one comes to see her. People are embarrassed by tragedies, you know, and the smell that remains in the air afterwards, cloaking the entire house."

"Hmm," I said shaking my head. I knew that Sara's mother had passed away almost a year ago, and that she had been ill for a few years before that. "Sara never speaks about her mother."

"Yes, the child was very young when her mother first got sick, so she's basically been without a mother for a very long time. I think that's why she's so attached to you now."

I raised an eyebrow as I thought about this. Sara was

indeed very attached to me, but I had attributed this to the fact that I was like an older sister, telling her stories and playing games with her.

"I thought it was because we spent so much time together."

"Of course it is," said Miranda, raising the thread to her mouth to snip it with her front teeth. She drew her lips back into a mock grimace so as not to moisten the thread, and in one quick bite, it was severed. Then she ran her fingers over the length of the thread, smoothing it out, and soon began stitching in a different location.

"Before you came, Sara was pretty quiet all the time, and she was not really interested in anyone or anything. Now she's skipping around the house and getting into trouble—things children normally do. So, you see, you've made a difference. We can all see it. And *Doña* Fabiola can see it too."

I looked up at Miranda. "But I thought that was a good thing. I thought that's what *Doña* Fabiola wanted," I said morosely.

Miranda bobbed her head softly, her eyes tracking her swiftly moving needle. "Well, it's complicated. She does and she doesn't. She wants her granddaughter to be happy, of course, but she's not thrilled that Sara seems to have forgotten her mother, *Doña* Fabiola's only daughter, so easily. I mean, I'm sure that Sara has not forgotten her mother, but seeing how happy she is with you makes *Doña* Fabiola feel cheated. Does that make sense?"

"You mean that it should have been her daughter making Sara feel good, not me," I said, twisting a lock of my hair around my finger. I had never thought of it that way before, but Miranda's explanation helped to make sense of *Doña* Fabiola's incessant hostility toward me. The whole time I had worked there I had been trying so hard to get on the old lady's good side.

I knew that she loved her granddaughter, so I was extra attentive to Sara—especially before she and I clicked and it came more naturally.

But now I could see that it was a paradox: the more I did, the less satisfied *Doña* Fabiola was. And if I did nothing at all, if I were to treat Sara with benevolent indifference, the grandmother would fire me. She had made that clear from the beginning. There was no way to win her affection or respect.

Doña Fabiola had lost her only daughter, and that had turned her into a bitter, drunk old lady. Sara had lost her mother and now she had lost her grandmother too, who was never sober enough to give her the attention or love that she needed. That's why Sara clung so tightly to me when I told her stories and took care of her. But seeing how Sara adored me made *Doña* Fabiola hate me and want to punish me.

Still, I knew better than to stand up to *Doña* Fabiola. In my previous job at a house in the neighboring village, I had seen one of the maids talk back to her unreasonable employer and the poor woman had been punched hard in the jaw and fired on the spot. I'm sure it took weeks, if not months, for her face to heal. I had vowed that I would never speak up that way and risk both the physical punishment and sudden irrevocable unemployment.

As I sat there thinking about all of this, I finished eating and then went to the bathroom to wash my fingers and rinse the small plate. As usual, I had not left a single grain of rice. I bent over the faucet and, making a cup with my hand, scooped several handfuls of cool water into my mouth. Then I wiped my hands and face on the thin cotton towel, and returned to the bedroom.

Miranda was still stitching the patch on her skirt. She had placed a small, brightly colored circle of fabric over the tiny hole, and fastened it with a few dainty stitches. Now she was artfully embroidering petals around it. It looked like a flower had accidentally fallen onto her skirt as Miranda brushed past one of

57

the blossom-laden bushes, and a tiny bloom had magically attached itself to her dress, becoming part of the fabric. I watched Miranda's art work with admiration.

"Will you be staying on for long in this household, Sesi?"

It was a question I had been asking myself more and more lately, and as I pondered it again, I looked away. I stared at the uneven cement floor, full of cracks and parts that were chipping away, as if even it was too exhausted to remain in this melancholy house, being stepped on day after day.

"I don't know," I said after a few moments. "I'm not sure whether *Doña* Fabiola will let me stay on as a *niñera* much longer, and I can see that she has no need for another servant."

Miranda chewed absently for a few seconds before she replied. She was still stitching at a steady pace. "Well, I hope you do stay, at least for a while. It's nice having you here. And, you know, it's not just Sara who likes your stories."

I looked up from floor and watched her face. Even though we had not known each other for that long, I had practically memorized the geography of it: her kind eyes, as dark as the craters of large, extinct volcanoes, and her aquiline nose, slightly crooked, as if the scars that raced across her left cheek had nudged it off its trajectory. Her hair was short and wavy and its color was the reddish brown that comes from being out in the sun and using caustic soap instead of shampoo.

"Thanks," I said, giving her a small smile.

"I'll teach you to cook. I really mean it."

I nodded. It was a promise Miranda had made several times before, and I knew that she did mean it, but there never seemed to be enough time.

"That would be great."

"Tomorrow. It's Saturday and I'll be making green rice. Come to the kitchen an hour before the rains begin and I'll teach you how to make green rice."

Chapter 6

El Salvador, 1959

Sesi

At around 2:00 p.m. the next day I went to the kitchen. The rest of the house was quiet now. The other two servants were working elsewhere—probably sweeping one of the four terracotta patios, a Sisyphean chore as there was always more dust in the air, more leaves and more bird droppings falling like errant missiles from some long-forgotten war, waiting for a nice clean floor to target. A local laborer, barefoot and bereft of his teeth, but not his smile, was languidly applying a fresh layer of white-wash to the cement wall outside of the living room.

Doña Fabiola, in a rare moment of inspiration, had gone into town to visit her sister, and Sara, whom I had cleaned up nicely, had been allowed to accompany her. Before they left, Sara had asked me to fix her hair a special way. She had been excited about her visit to her grand aunt's house and it had been difficult to make her hair behave as she wiggled back and forth in her glee.

"I'm sure we'll stop for some green mangoes," she told me as I worked on her hair. We both loved the crunchy mangoes soaked in sour lemon juice and sprinkled with large crystals of sea salt.

"You're a funny little bird, Sara. You don't want to eat

60

your food at home," I chided gently, "and then you beg for these treats. That's not good."

Sara pouted briefly but I knew that she would probably manage to convince her grandmother to stop and purchase the treat. It was a small miracle that she did not become very sick from eating food sold in the street, very possibly contaminated from unclean hands, but I said nothing. As I worked on her hair, twisting it around so that it lay elegantly atop her head and fastening it with pins, I told her a tale about a mermaid who had gotten lost on her way home from a party with some very handsome blue dolphins.

Don Enrique had gone somewhere—a meeting, a bar, a brothel—one could never tell as he returned from all of them similarly drunk and in a comparably foul mood. Of course, no one questioned his comings and goings, and he didn't make his schedule public.

Miranda was already working in the kitchen when I arrived. She handed me a clean but rather dismal apron that bore indelible, semi-transparent grease splatters, orange tomato sauce stains and brownish-black burn marks. Once my apron was secured around my waist, she nodded to a knife and a cutting board sitting on the counter next to three round green peppers, each smaller than an orange, and a large onion. I peeled and chopped with the clumsiness of a novice, wiping my eyes with the corners of my apron when the onion overpowered me, and trying not to complain. I knew that I had to learn this skill to survive in my next job, so I kept at it diligently.

As we worked, we chatted.

"When I went to buy the peppers at the market this morning, I ran into Auxiliadora, you know, she works for the house down the street there," said Miranda motioning in the direction of the house in question with a quick cock of her head.

"The house with the big lemon tree in the front?"

61

"That one. And she told me the funniest story. She said a bat flew in during the night and knocked down the knickknacks that the family had on top of their china cabinet. When the family heard the noise they came running, thinking it was an intruder. Auxiliadora was in her night dress and she was very frightened but she turned on the light and there was the bat, flying all around the room. *Doña* Gabriela came in and saw it too. She told Auxiliadora to turn the light back off and then she opened the big window on the far end of the room and the bat flew back out."

I shuddered involuntarily at the thought of a bat entering my room. There was no glass in the windows, so a bat could easily come in at any time. But they usually didn't, which I felt fortunate about. *Doña* Laura later told me that all windows in the houses in the land where she comes from had glass, and although that seemed nice, it also made me a bit sad for the people who wouldn't naturally have the lovely breezes blowing through the house but would always have to remember to open and close the windows.

"When you've got all the green peppers and onions chopped up, you put them into the blender like this, see?" she said, stepping aside to be sure I had not missed seeing the process. Miranda was a careful teacher, breaking down the recipe into baby steps that she demonstrated to me, one by one.

I had brought a small piece of paper and a pencil stub to write the recipe down, but she seemed not to trust that I was paying attention if I wasn't looking directly at her operations. That's why every time I put my head down to write, she felt that she needed to get my attention again.

"And then you add the water, see?" Miranda said, carefully pouring the water over the green chunks in the glass blender jar. "Like this, see, and then you push this button here, the middle one, and you keep your finger pressed hard on it until you can see that everything is chopped up to tiny bits. If you take your finger off too soon, the green peppers will still be chunky."

As she spoke, the blades of the blender whirled to life, making a strong purring sound, and soon a green, frothy mixture had emerged from the peppers and water. It was very nice to watch how quickly the blades chopped the peppers to smithereens. I could imagine that in the olden days, when the Pilpil Indians ruled the land, the cooks must have had to spend hours chopping and mashing to create this mixture that modern machinery engendered in just seconds.

"Now you add your cream," she said, gently pouring the thick white liquid over the mixture, "and your parsley and olive oil, and you mix again."

The mixture now turned a light mint-green color. I was watching carefully. Cooks were generally paid more than regular *muchachas*, or *niñeras*. I had been a *muchacha* before, and the work had been tedious.

A fly buzzed in, circling and whirling in an annoying manner, occasionally landing on my arm as I tried to work. I shooed it away, but it kept returning and running up my forearm, like I was a tall jungle tree it wanted to scale, or across my neck, tickling me along its trajectory. Then it flew to Miranda and that was its fatal mistake because she immediately took action. She walked to the corner of the kitchen and reached for a piece of newspaper which she kept in a stack.

Old newspapers were her go-to material. She used them to catch peelings, wipe surfaces, mop up things, wrap things, kill things and dispose of things. I paused for a moment to watch Miranda as she expertly folded several sheets together and then rolled them into the shape of a cone. She waved it at the fly, who was pestering me again, and when it landed on a wall a second later, she whacked it. Then she tore a corner of the newspaper off and gingerly picked up the dead bug and threw it back out the window.

Flies, which we call *moscas*, congregated in many of the rooms of the house, often three, four or five at time, dancing an elliptical fly dance in the center of the rooms, as if they were trying to conjure up small tornados. However, if any of them wandered into the kitchen, well, that was the end of them. Miranda's kitchen was *mosca non grata* territory.

"Meanwhile, you've got your rice here, in the pan, frying gently in some oil with a bit of finely chopped onions and some carrots," Miranda said, picking up her conversation where she had set it aside before the fly incident.

"With no water?" I asked. "I thought rice was supposed to be cooked with water?"

Miranda shook her head. "You'll add the water in a bit. But you have to let the raw rice grains toast in the oil first so they can absorb the goodness of the onions."

"And you just measured the rice straight from the bag?" I asked. I had meant to be in the kitchen when Miranda first began fixing the typical green rice dinner, but Sara's hair had taken a bit longer than I had anticipated.

"No, you can never use rice straight from the bag," said Miranda. "Here, look."

She took my hand and poured a small amount of rice into it and I saw that there were tiny twigs and a few small rocks and debris mixed among the grains of rice.

"See? The rice is dirty so you have to sort through it first, then you rinse it, and then you fry it to draw out its goodness."

I put the rice carefully back into the bag while Miranda grabbed the jug from the blender and walked to the pan of rice. I peeked into the pan and saw that the rice grains were dancing around because of the heat, and turning pale brown, while the

64

onion softened and became translucent.

"Then you add this mixture," Miranda said, "Always two cups of liquid for each cup of rice."

I counted six cups of the green pepper and parsley mixture with Miranda. Then I watched as she slowly stirred the rice into the soupy green liquid.

"Now you add the chicken bouillon," she said, and withdrew 3 shiny cubes from a jar. She quickly unwrapped them, discarding the foil, and crushed them with her strong fingers before putting them into the rice mixture. "You stir just a bit now, then you put your spoon down and you don't stir that pot again," said Miranda with finality. I felt like she was scolding me for something I had not done.

I peered into the pot at the neat grains rolling slightly as bubbles of liquid jostled them. "What would happen if I stirred the rice?"

"Stirring rice makes it get sticky, and you don't want that. If you don't stir any more, it won't get ruined. Many people make this mistake. You need to trust the rice and let it do its own thing."

I liked that advice as it seemed to me that it could apply to a lot of situations, so I turned back to my small piece of paper and dutifully wrote down Miranda's words.

Miranda watched me curiously for a moment, and then she said, "So how is it that you know how to read and write? Did you go to school past eight?"

Only three years of education were mandatory across the country, and while boys often stayed in schools longer, most girls were pulled from school at the end of third grade to help with the chores and to keep them from dangerous men. It was a fact of life in all parts of the country, not just the village where I had been raised, that young girls were in very real danger of being kidnapped and raped on their way to or from school, so most girls were pulled out before then to protect them.

"I learned how to read from my brother."

"He taught you? How nice! That's rather unusual, isn't it?"

"No, he didn't teach me. At least not on purpose. My mother didn't want me to learn how to read and write because she said girls didn't need that."

Miranda nodded. "My mother said the same thing."

"And did you have older brothers?" I asked, realizing that I had never asked this question in all the months we had been together.

"I only had younger sisters," said Miranda. "Two of them died as babies, but one still lives."

I lowered my eyes out of respect. It was a fact of life in this country: most children had a difficult time making it to their first birthday, but if they got that far, they fared all right.

"I'm sorry," I said.

"It happens," she said with resignation. "Go on."

"Well, I really wanted to learn to read," I explained. "I think I wanted it more than he did. So as I washed the dishes in the afternoon, when he came home from school, I could hear him recite his reading practice. You know, 'B + A = BA; C + A = CA' and things like that. When he said it, I would repeat it quietly, working hard to memorize everything. Then at night, when he and my mother were asleep, I would take his book and go outside. When the moon was at least a quarter full, there was enough light to see and I would memorize everything. If it was too dark, I would light a candle. I had a small stick that I would use like a pencil, and I would scratch the letters into the soil. When I finished, I would smear it all around to erase my work.

"My mother never caught me and I never told her that I was reading."

Miranda nodded, her astonishment showing. "You were brave."

"I was stubborn," I said. "I wanted to read so badly. I thought it was like magic, being able to take meaning from marks on a piece of paper. It hasn't gotten me much, but it does help. Like now. I can write this down and I'll remember it."

"Have you ever read a book?" Miranda asked.

I shook my head. "I read my brother's workbooks, when I could get them. Some had little stories. But I have never read a whole book. I read articles and notices in the newspaper. I read all the signs and billboards. And one day I will read a book. That's my plan."

Miranda nodded, appreciatively. "Do you think you could teach me too? I mean, I might be too old to learn..."

"I'd be happy to," I said, delighted to be able to pay her back for her gift of teaching me the valuable skill of cooking. "I have an idea. You can teach me to cook more foods and I'll teach you to read. We'll trade!"

Miranda smiled and it made her scars look friendly. She approached the stove again, and motioned for me to join her.

"Look at this now," she said. "See how the water level is going down? Can you tell that it is much lower than it was just a few minutes ago? When the water gets below the level of the rice, you take a small spoon and scoop the rice from the edges up to the center like this, making a volcano."

She worked the outer ring of the pot, heaping the rice gently into the center and soon a small, steep-sided mountain began to form. "By doing this, the steam will continue to cook it and you can see where the water level is. When it gets to the bottom of the pan, you need to shut the fire off and put a folded clean cloth over the top so that it can sit for..."

Just then the swinging kitchen door burst open.

"What the hell! I thought I heard talking in the kitchen!"

It was *Doña* Fabiola. How had she come back so soon from the visit with her sister? I had not expected her and Sara to return until dinner.

"What are you doing in here, girl?" she said, practically spitting at me.

"I...I was just leaving, *Doña* Fabiola," I said, lowering my head and exiting the kitchen by the back entrance, in the direction of the back patio of the house, where the servant rooms were. I had quickly tucked the tiny scrap of paper and my small pencil into the pocket of my apron as soon as the door swung open.

"And you, when will dinner be ready?" I could hear her saying to Miranda. Anyone could have heard her as she was still screaming.

"Very soon now, *señora*," said Miranda.

I could tell from her voice that she was also frightened.

"Well, hopefully that *puta* hasn't ruined it or eaten everything. She's a bad one, that Sesi. I don't know why I keep her in this house. My generosity is lethal! Bah!" She left the kitchen, still muttering to herself.

A few minutes later I crept back into the kitchen. Miranda saw me and warned me that the coast was not clear by raising her eyebrows and motioning to the other door, flicking her eyes in that direction. I took a deep breath and held it as I tip-toed across the room and listened at the swinging door for a moment. Then I very gently pushed the door open a fraction and looked out into the dining room. It was empty. I silently went through the doors and out into the dining room, and then the hallway, peering all around, just in case the old woman was lurking close by. In a few moments I returned to the kitchen.

"She must have gone to bed. I can't believe she's drunk so early in the afternoon," I said in a soft voice.

Miranda nodded. "How long can you stay here?"

I looked outside. The rains were just beginning which meant that it was 3:00. "I'll have to go give Sara her afternoon snack now. How is the rice?"

She lifted a corner of the cloth from the top of the pan, and a cloud of savory steam escaped, revealing the creamy green rice dish.

I shook my head in admiration—it was impressive how she could make the food so wonderfully. "It smells delicious!" I said.

Miranda nodded and went to the refrigerator to get out the meat. "Do you want to watch me cook the rest of the dinner?"

"No. I mean, I do, but I'd better not. The old lady might get up again. We'll catch up tonight and you can tell me what you did. Oh, and see if you can find some blank paper and you'll have your first writing lesson too."

Chapter 7

El Salvador, 1959

Sesi

"I know we are just servants, but we're living in modern times now, and things should be getting better, don't you think? I mean, the world should be becoming a better place," Miranda declared.

We were sitting at the small, wooden table in the corner of the kitchen, speaking softly. *Doña* Fabiola had finished her dinner, dishes had been cleared and now the servants were eating. The other two preferred to eat in the back courtyard of the house, the one where laundry was hung to dry. It had a cement floor which sloped to the center where a round, rusting drain grate adorned the middle of the floor like a medallion. The shingled roof of the house extended a few feet over the edge where the wall met the roof, forming a shaded area during the day, and that's where some plastic chairs and a small card table had been placed. It was already dark now, but still the two servants liked to be out there.

I suppose that eating there gave them more privacy to talk and gossip because in the kitchen, you could never be absolutely sure that no one was in the dining room, sneaking up on you. But Miranda's territory was the kitchen and it's where she was happiest, so I joined her there.

70

I was keeping an eye on the clock, which I wound dutifully every morning, as I would need to leave shortly to get Sara. I had another half hour. It was unusual for Sara to play at a friend's house and stay for dinner—*Don* Enrique usually said no to the few invitations she got—but this invitation had slipped in like a bat in the night, sneaking in late this afternoon while *Don* Enrique was out. *Doña* Fabiola had been in a rare, generous mood. So I had taken Sara, who was bubbling with joy, to her friend's house.

Miranda finished her tortilla and licked her fingertips, making sure to get every bit of flavor. Then she wiped her fingers on her apron. It was an old one, for wearing around the house, not a nice one that she would wear if she had to run an errand or if there were guests in the house.

"The world is a better place than it used to be," I said. "We have running water. I don't have to go to the stream to get water every morning. And we have an indoor bathroom. That's better." I wasn't kidding either. Running water and an indoor bathroom were still small miracles as far as I was concerned.

Miranda looked at me. "You rarely ever talk about your past, Sesi. Why did you leave home? Are your parents still alive?"

I couldn't hold her gaze. "I...well, I never really knew my father," I said in a quiet voice. Speaking of him made me sad. "My mother says he was a nice man, but he just wasn't able to support us. It embarrassed him, so he left."

"Any uncles?"

"Two, but one died in an accident when I was little."

She cocked her head at me.

"He was helping with construction, I think they were building the church, and a brick or something fell on his foot. Something really heavy. It got infected and they said he needed

71

to go to a hospital and have it amputated. He refused and then the poison spread through his body and he died."

Miranda winced. "I've heard of that happening," she said. It felt good to hear her affirmation

"I don't remember any of it. And my mother, well, you know how it is. She didn't really have the money to support me."

Miranda understood. Once a daughter reached the age of twelve, she was fully employable and it was common for *muchachas* to live in the houses where they worked. Having me gone was a great financial relief to my mother.

"Yeah, me too," said Miranda. "I manage to send some money home a few times a year to help out the old lady."

I smiled. "I do too, but it's never enough. One of our neighbors, Linda, went to work in San Salvador. She's four years older than me and she sends home much more money than I ever do. My mother is always quick to point this out. That's why I'm making my way to the capital city. I'll be able to get more money there."

The fact that I could have a conversation like this with Miranda shows you how close we were. I never really spoke with anyone, mostly because people weren't really ever interested in hearing what I wanted to say. People wanted to be heard, but they didn't want to listen. I learned that pretty quick when I left home so I mostly listened and it kept me out of trouble. But with Miranda, it was different. She was balanced in her talking and listening departments.

"San Salvador? Aren't you afraid?" she said, chewing on a thin branch that she had picked earlier in the day. It was fragrant and it poked out on the right side of her mouth, where she had more teeth. I found myself wondering if in ten years, when I was as old as she was, I would also gnaw on sticks.

"That's a really big city and it's dangerous there," she

said, finishing her thought, as if she had been chewing on it as well.

I reflected on the question while I rubbed my fingers along the tines of my fork, feeling their smooth tapered prongs and poking my fingertips gently into the tips. Then I examined the skewed row of dots on my fingertips. This was because the tines were bent. It was oddly cathartic to cause these impressions in my finger tips and I often found myself playing with forks that way. It was kind of like biting my lips, that feeling of manageable pain.

"I guess," I said, shrugging my shoulders. "But I'll have to go there when I'm older anyway. It's the only place where I'll always have work. And I'll be ready to work in a big city by then."

Miranda shook her head. I'm sorry that *Doña* Fabiola yells at you so much.

"It's okay. I'm used to it," I said, my glance sliding from Miranda's face to the bright mass of bougainvillea flowers growing outside. As in our bedroom, there was no glass in the small holes that were built into the wall to serve as windows. It was like the house had a bunch of small mouths that allowed it to breathe so it wouldn't get too hot or stuffy inside. Other windows in the house had small glass panes that could be rolled open or shut, but in areas considered to be 'servant territory,' none of the windows had glass. Most of the time this was a good thing.

Miranda nodded. "Well, it's not right. I mean, I know she went crazy after her daughter's death, but she didn't used to pick on people so much the way she does now."

"It's not so bad," I said, trying to make her feel better. Sometimes Miranda could look so sad. "I keep my head down and don't answer back."

"I noticed that you do that, and that's good. If you fought

with her, she would have fired you by now."

Outside the window, an enormous flock of hundreds of wild *pericos* was flying overhead, chattering loudly. They swooped and landed in the trees, descending like dark rain clouds on the black wires that zig-zagged back and forth between wooden poles. They were squawking so loudly that we almost had trouble hearing our own thoughts. Then, all at once, they rose into the air and flew off, leaving a hollow silence in their wake.

"Miranda, what happened to the girl that was here before me?"

She stopped chewing and stared straight ahead, lost in thought.

"*Don* Enrique got to her," she said, very quietly.

"He yelled at her a lot?"

Miranda shook her head.

"He got her pregnant."

I covered my mouth with both my hands.

"At least, that's what I suspect. She never said. But he would come home drunk and I'm pretty sure he attacked her. She would come back to the room, after it was dark, shaking. Always on nights when he was drunk and asked her to serve him dinner. They would disappear together. Then I would see the bruises on her arms and thighs."

"What...what did she say?"

Miranda stared ahead again, as if she had slipped into another world. I waited, being careful not to breathe too loudly lest I disturb her thoughts.

"She never said anything. She was only thirteen," Miranda whispered.

"Poor thing!"

"Yeah, it got pretty bad. A girl barely older than his own daughter. Shame on him. But shame on me too. I guessed what was going on and I should have helped her. I should have asked her to confide in me. I should have told her to run away. But I guess she didn't really have anywhere to go anyway," said Miranda, and the sadness and remorse in her voice flowed thick like lava.

I kept both my hands on my face, and I could feel my cheeks getting really hot. I wanted her to tell me more but I was too scared to ask so I just sat still. A fly buzzed into the room and Miranda's eyes flicked toward her pile of newspapers in the corner, but before she made the move to get up, the fly found its way back out. Lucky fly.

"When she started showing *Doña* Fabiola fired her. She accused Blanca of being a slut, sleeping around. I don't really know what happened with her or her baby after they left here."

"Didn't *Doña* Fabiola know what *Don* Enrique was doing? Why didn't Blanca tell her that it was her grandchild she was carrying?"

Miranda tsked, and shook her head several times as she ran her finger over the edge of the table. "No, well, it wouldn't have been her grandchild, would it? I mean, *Don* Enrique is her son-in-law."

I studied the cracks in the cement floor. So many cracks, once you started looking. Floors, lives, everywhere there were cracks. Even the planet had cracks, people said, and that's why it shook from time to time. Ours was a cracked and flawed world.

"But even if *Don* Enrique were her son, there's no way *Doña* Fabiola would acknowledge an out-of-wedlock child with a servant, would she?" Miranda said.

I wagged my head slightly, still not raising my eyes from

75

the intricate patterns on the ground. Even though I had asked, I now felt very uneasy speaking about this situation.

"So that afternoon, when *Doña* Fabiola realized that Blanca was pregnant, she sent her packing right then and there. I managed to give her a few *colones*, which was all the money that I had, and a little bit of food. I whispered to Blanca to come back after dark and check the hollow of a tree where I tucked them."

"And did she?"

Miranda raised an eyebrow and shrugged. Then she spat out the bit of twig she'd been chewing on. "Maybe she did, or maybe some other poor soul got to it before her. I never saw her again."

I remained pensive for a moment. It was so unfair. But that was the way life was, I realized. Fairness was not a concept that life understood.

There was something else I should have thought, and I didn't. I should have realized that men like *Don* Enrique are volcanoes, quiet for a while, but you can never really be sure they are extinct, and they might suddenly erupt at any time. I was like the cricket in the garage, chirping happily, not realizing that my very existence was enough to turn the underside of a shoe in my direction.

Chapter 8

El Salvador, 1959

Sesi

"Tell me about when you were little, Sesi," Sara demanded. It was the end of another day, about two months after I'd had that conversation with Miranda in the kitchen. I was tucking Sara into bed and I wasn't surprised at her open-ended question. She always tried to find a way to delay the moment when I would shut off her light and leave her for the night.

"Oh, I was never little," I said, teasing her. "I was always just as big as I am now." I pulled the light blanket and sheet up to her neck but she wriggled her arms back out.

"No, you weren't! Everyone was little once. Even you!"

"How do you know?" I asked, raising one eyebrow. "Have you ever known me to be anything different than I am now?"

Sara crinkled her forehead as she thought, then promptly changed the subject.

"I wrote your name in my notebook today," she said. "I wrote: 'Sesi is the best story teller in the whole world,' and then I showed it to my teacher and she said that I did it wrong. She said your name is spelled 'C-E-C-I' but I told her that you showed me that it was 'S-E-S-I.' She said 'Ceci' was short for Cecilia, with a

'C.' Is that true? Is that your real name?"

I smiled. It had been ages since anyone had said my full name. "Actually, she's right in a way," I said and saw her face fall, "and she's wrong in another way. 'Cecilia' is my full name and it is spelled that way, but I changed my name when I was little."

"You did? Why?"

I thought for a moment. It wasn't like people went around writing my name all the time in newspapers or books, so it didn't really matter. "I guess I liked the shape of the 'S' better. It's more fancy and artistic than a 'C' which just looks like a big mouth ready to swallow something. So when I was little, I decided that my name was spelled that way, and that's how I've done it ever since."

Sara nodded, her eyes struggling to stay open. "Sara starts with an 'S' too, so you and me both have pretty shaped letters to start our names," she said, yawning.

"That's right, and that makes us both very special people," I said and stood up. "Time to sleep now."

"But I want a story!" she said, blinking to wake herself up.

"I've already told you a story, young lady," I said gently, reaching for the lamp. I knew she would be asleep in no time. "And now you need to get your beauty sleep, so you're nice and cheerful tomorrow and ready for school."

"But..."

"You heard what she said," said a masculine voice from behind me. Both Sara and I were startled and looked to see *Don* Enrique's silhouette at the door. He entered the room and came to stand behind me, surreptitiously placing his hand over my buttocks. I immediately stiffened, but did not want to react more in front of Sara. *Don* Enrique must have known that that was

78

what I would do, so he calmly kept his hand in place and increased the pressure.

"Now, be a good girl and I'm sure..." he looked toward me and suddenly Sara realized that he did not know my name. I had been in that house for the better part of a year and he had never spoken to me.

"Sesi, Papá, this is Sesi. She's my best friend and she spells her name with an 'S' just like me!"

"Sesi, right. I'm sure Sesi will tell you more stories tomorrow, like she promised." He released my buttocks and I immediately stepped away from him. *Don* Enrique approached his daughter and bent down, lowering his face to Sara's so that she could kiss his cheek, and then he shut off the lamp on Sara's bedside table.

I retreated quickly and had already reached the door when I felt his iron hand on my wrist. We exited the room and he forcefully pulled me down the hall. I resisted as much as I dared, making some scuffling sounds, but feared both disturbing Sara and engendering anger in *Don* Enrique, who I realized smelled very strongly of whisky and cigar smoke. I was desperately afraid that he would hurt me more if I fought him.

He forced me into his bedroom, where the light was on and a newspaper lay, half-read, on his rumpled bed. To my horror and great distress, he immediately began tearing at my dress with his free hand, while still pinning my wrist painfully behind me. I twisted and struggled, pushing and trying to kick him as best as I could, but I was no match for him. He was much larger and stronger, and he was holding me tightly, whispering filthy names at me and insisting that I hold still before we woke up anyone. We!

I tried another kick but he pushed me ruthlessly backwards and I slammed into the closet door, my head making a sickening crack. The wooden door was a bit loose in its rails so the sound was pretty loud, but I was focusing on the daggers of pain that were shooting into my brain and flashes of light rocketing through the air in front of me.

Suddenly he froze as we heard a voice at the door.

"*Don* Enrique?" said *Doña* Fabiola.

I would have tried to scream but suddenly his big, sweaty hand was forced over my mouth, covering my nose as well. I felt even more panic, thinking he would suffocate me. My head was still searing with pain and I could feel a warm trickle of blood running down the back of my neck.

"*Don* Enrique, are you in there? I wanted to ask you about..." the door pushed open and suddenly *Doña* Fabiola was standing there looking at us.

For a long second *Doña* Fabiola's eyes darted between us. She took in my half-torn dress and disheveled hair. As if suddenly waking from a dream, *Don* Enrique forcefully pushed me away and I fell to the floor. I was so ashamed that I kept my eyes down.

"*Puta!*" said *Doña* Fabiola in a lethally quiet voice. "Get out of this house right now! This poor man, his wife's body not even cold in the grave and you're already scheming to get him into bed. I knew you were a good-for-nothing whore! Out of here, right now. Go pack your bags and leave tonight."

I was too stunned and too relieved to say anything. I scrambled to my knees and stumbled out of the room, then ran blindly back to the bedroom I shared with Miranda.

Chapter 9

El Salvador, 1959

Sesi

"*Don* Enrique got you," Miranda gasped when she saw me, and her hands flew up to her mouth. She pulled me into the room, closing the door behind me.

She found a rag and cleaned up the cut on the back of my head, which thankfully, was no longer bleeding. As she worked, I related the events of the last few minutes to her in whispered tones. Then she told me to take a quick shower.

When I emerged a few minutes later, I saw that she had taken my dress and was hastily stitching up the tears.

I took my other dress down from the nail and put it on. Then I gathered my scant belongings into a plastic bag.

"I'd better leave now," I said in a hushed voice. My throat was full of rough pebbles.

"I really hate to see you go, Sesi," said Miranda, her eyes swimming with tears.

I nodded but didn't say anything.

The house was eerily quiet. Not even the crickets were chirping. I was pretty sure that outside of me and *Doña* Fabiola and *Don* Enrique, no one had heard what had occurred.

Fortunately, Sara was asleep. I figured it was best if I could just get out as quickly as possible.

"Where will you go?"

"I'm going to get a job in San Salvador someday. For now, I'll just head in that direction and stop at the next place that needs me."

"Do you think you'll be a *niñera* again?"

I shrugged. "Don't know. I'll try, but if I can't, I'll work as a *muchacha*."

Miranda stood and gave me a hug. "Go with God," she said, stuffing my mended dress into the bag with my other belongings. "And may the Virgin keep you close to her bosom on your journey. But for tonight, go to the Parque Mirasol, close to the forest. You know where that is? Good. You'll find a big statue of a horse there. If you follow the direction that his head is pointing, about twenty paces or so, you'll get to a big clump of bamboo stalks. Go to the edge of the stalks and feel around until you find a part where you can squeeze in between them. Once you are inside, head toward the center of the clump. It'll be tight going for a bit, but eventually you'll see a small space there where you can lie down and spend the night safely."

I thanked her and took my bag.

"I'll always remember your kindness, Miranda. May God bless you, too."

She hugged me one more time. "One more thing: if you come back tomorrow, after midday, I'll sneak some food into the old mango tree, by the corner of the block, in a little hollow it has, just above eye-level. Reach in and take it, but don't come any closer to the house."

I felt my heart expand in wonder and gratitude. I did not voice either of these sentiments, though. There was no need. The poor always helped each other in any way we could. It was what

82

we did.

"Will you be all right?" I asked her.

She raised her hand to her face, grazing her scars as she spoke. "Sure, I suppose, and if not, I'll leave too. I'm lucky that *Don* Enrique doesn't fancy me. It's because of these scars on my face. They are my lucky charm."

I looked at Miranda, holding her gaze. In all the time I had known her, I had never thought of her scars as a good thing. When I first met her, I felt sorry for her. Then I stopped noticing them as much. I knew there were people who were repelled by her scars. I guess in the back of my mind she was like the Monkey Princess, making her way the best that she could with the cruel fate that had been handed down to her. But now I realized that instead of a curse, her scars were her box of lucky matches, protecting her.

"And don't you think *Doña* Fabiola doesn't know the truth about you," Miranda added, her whispered voice lowering even further.

"The truth?" I was bewildered by Miranda's declaration. What truth? Did Miranda also believe that I had been trying to seduce *Don* Enrique? Did everyone think I was a...I couldn't even finish the thought. It was too horrible for words.

"She knows that he was trying to hurt you tonight. And she knows that you were helping Sara, even though it reminds her of her loss. Don't you see. She never goes into his bedroom like that, after dark, like she did tonight. She must have heard the tussle and gone to investigate. I bet she was even expecting it to happen at some point, like it did with Blanca. Yes, that's it! And she was protecting you by banishing you so frequently. I never connected the dots until now, but several of those times that she sent you to our room without dinner, right afterwards, *Don* Enrique stumbled into the kitchen, more than half drunk, looking for more food. I think she knew that he was on the prowl, and that he would not be attracted to me. Don't you see?"

I started to shake my head, but then I did remember that he was always in the background when she yelled at me and that Miranda was probably right. The old lady didn't hate me. She was rescuing me. And by constantly proclaiming loudly that I was no good, she was hoping to keep him off my scent. It really turned my world upside down to think about it, I tell you, and with the fright I'd had, it was all I could do to stay on my feet.

"I think she also knew about Blanca," said Miranda, pensively. "And I think she feels guilty that she never did anything to stop it. I guess it was too soon after her daughter's death and she was still fighting her own demons of grief. We all were. But keep in mind that she told you to pack your bags. If she really thought you were bad, she would have sent you off with nothing. I've seen her do that before. She sent off other *muchachas* without allowing them to pack their few belongings when she got mad at them. She can be ruthless. If she really had thought that you were a slut, you would already be in the street right now. And she might have called the police and made sure you were in big trouble. Or she might have stayed outside the door and let him rape you."

I shivered at the thought. Miranda was right. Before tonight I had thought that *Doña* Fabiola hated me and that I was a nuisance in her life. But I had completely misunderstood the situation.

"Thanks for everything," I said again, and then took my shopping bag and left the house, as quietly as a salamander. I was heading out into the dark night all by myself, but it was not as dark as it would have been if Miranda had not shared her light-filled thoughts with me.

Chapter 10

Illinois, 1959

Laura

Laura made the best of her last few years at home, but life on the farm was demanding and her mother's anger was always simmering, just below the surface. One afternoon, Laura came home early from hunting. She was walking quietly with her dog, Pointer, when he suddenly went stiff and lifted his paw. She followed his gaze and saw that the barn door was nearly closed, which was unusual for that time of day.

A tingling feeling ran up her spine and she walked very quietly in the direction of the barn. She stood still for a few seconds and then she heard tussling and a small yelp. There were no animals kept there, so she immediately guessed what was happening. She motioned for Pointer to stay as she ran the last few paces to the door.

"Hey, what's going on?" she said in a loud voice. The big, heavy door was nearly shut, but she pushed it open and light flowed in, like water on parched land. She heard a few more muffled noises and pushed the door the rest of the way open, aiming her shotgun inside. It took a moment for her eyes to adjust to the shadows, but what she saw broke her heart. Her little sister was getting up from the ground, red in the face and dusting hay off her dress. Long strands of her hair were pulled

85

out of its ponytail, and she was shaking.

"What happened?" Laura asked, looking around for her father. She knew he must be hiding somewhere nearby.

"Nothing," said her sister. "I…I must have tripped."

It was an unconvincing lie.

"Come here," said Laura, scolding herself for not having thought of it earlier. She put her arm around her sister and the two walked out to the apple grove.

"Was it Pop?" she asked quietly when they were far from the barn.

Sally looked down at the ground and a tear ran down her bright red cheek.

"You're coming hunting with me and Jimmy tomorrow," said Laura. "That'll put a stop to that."

Sally wrapped her arms tightly around Laura's waist and shook with sobs for several minutes.

"Shh, it's going to be all right," said Laura, patting her back.

"I owe you," said Sally gratefully, leaning her head on Laura's shoulder as they walked.

"Nonsense," said Laura. "Sisters stick together."

That evening Laura fashioned a sling for her shotgun and began wearing it indoors.

"That's not for wearing around inside the house," said her mother, looking at her askance.

"Sally saw the coyote right outside the window this afternoon. It scared her pretty bad. We've got to be ready at all times to shoot it. It's the only way, Mom. I've taught Sally how to shoot and she'll get him good the next time he comes anywhere near the farm," said Laura in her most reasonable voice. She didn't look at her father, but out of the corner of her eye she saw him hunch down farther behind his newspaper.

When Laura finished her homework and her chores, she and Sally would practice target shooting in a visible location. It was Sally's idea to save an extra shot aimed at a noisy tin can for right about the time their father came in from the fields. Laura had her shotgun with her at all times, sometimes even at the breakfast table. And her plan worked flawlessly: her father had never touched either of the girls again.

The two sisters spent as much time as possible with their cousin Jimmy, fishing, hunting for squirrels and rabbits and swimming in the watering hole. There were times that Laura even imagined that she was in love with Jimmy and she would wonder if he felt the same way. He called them his best pals and she rather liked the sound of that. But things changed her senior year when he began dating Darleen. After that he made it pretty clear that he didn't want his cousins tagging along.

Chapter 11

El Salvador, 1959

Sesi

"Sesi, wake up! Shhh! Wake up now, it's getting late," said Miranda.

I opened my eyes, still groggy. Long, scary hours had passed since I had last heard her friendly voice. I had been very frightened when I first got to the park and had panicked when I got close to the statue and saw another shadow, but it turned out to be nothing. I found the horse, circled the fountain until I was in front of its head and then walked twenty paces. But the bamboo patch was farther away. Then it had taken me a while to find the opening into the thicket and to navigate my way toward the center. There I had made a nest on the ground among the rough bamboo leaves which made a surprising amount of noise as I settled myself down and tried to sleep. But sleep had taken a long time to find me in my new bed.

Every time the stalks shivered in the wind, they sounded like old bones rattling together. Or like someone was coming to get me. Had someone who saw me walking down the street followed me there? Had one of the homeless men sleeping in another part of the park seen me? Was he waiting until I started to doze off before he came for me?

There had been the other night noises which had also

88

startled me. The loud, insistent crickets were not disturbing as I heard them every night of my life through the open windows. It was the other sounds, the ones made by the city which should have been sleeping, that terrified me. There were dogs barking and I worried that one of them would sniff me out and either bite me or alert someone to my presence. There was also maniacal laughter from some drunken men, singing and shouting at each other. There were cars and trucks coming and going on the street not far from the park and I worried that their bright headlights would penetrate the thicket and reveal me, lying on the ground, vulnerable. There were even some loud noises that sounded like gun shots.

My mind was also having a field day coming up with frightening ideas. What if *Don* Enrique had seen me leave and had followed me? What if he was entering the thicket, right now, ready to have his way with me? Was that the wind or was it a footstep? And what if there were snakes here? Or big, poisonous spiders? Or fire ants? Or scorpions?

I was so tired that I even began imagining that there were dark spirits visiting me, just like the evil monkey spirit that had taken notice of Mariángeles. I knew I wasn't pretty enough to attract the ones that would want to marry me, but my overactive imagination came up with plenty of other nasty scenarios from which I wanted to escape. Eventually I must have managed to find sleep.

"Sesi, there's not much time. I've got to get back. I just wanted to give you this."

I sat up and looked at Miranda. The light around us was still gray as the sun had not yet risen, though the noises from the evening before were now gone.

"Here's twenty *colones*."

My eyes bulged. It was a small fortune! I could not let her part with that much money! I shook my head, no, pushing the

89

money back towards her.

"It's not mine. It's *Don* Enrique's."

"But..."

"Don't tell me it's stealing. He doesn't know the money is missing. I've been taking a little bit every now and then, ever since I found out about Blanca. It's retribution, you know. He never misses the money as he loses track of how much he has when he goes out drinking. But since he tried to hurt you, you deserve it. I've still got some left too, in case I need to leave in a hurry. I should have given it to you last night, but I didn't think of it, what with you needing to rush off like that. Put it inside your dress, yes, right there, next to your breast.

"Keep it there and never let anyone see it. If you have to spend any money to buy food, go to a private place and take out a few bills and put them in your pocket so you can spend them. But never let anyone see how much you have, all right? Good. Now, stand up and let me brush you off. Here, let's re-braid your hair," she said, turning me around and finger combing out my long braid before efficiently re-doing it. We didn't have much room there in the center of the bamboo stalks, but it had been enough for me to curl up, and it was enough to let us stand and visit quietly as she helped me prepare for my journey.

No one had done my hair in so long and I felt the way Sara must have felt on many mornings when I insisted on re-shaping her ponytails. It was both comforting and uncomfortable. It was nice to have someone caring for me, but part of me resented the idea of not doing it for myself.

"Now, off you go, my sweet little Sesi. It's better for you to leave before the rest of the city gets up. I've brought you the food I promised so you don't have to try to go to the mango tree later on. And here's a little knife to peel your food. You know what mango trees look like, so you won't go hungry."

90

I looked at Miranda in wonder. "Won't you get in trouble for not being home now?"

"I'm at the market, getting fresh eggs for breakfast," she said, kissing my cheek.

"I can never repay your generosity to me..."

"Hush, that's not true. You have already given me so much. You told me stories and taught me to read. I'm going to keep practicing and maybe someday I can save up enough money to open up my own restaurant, just like Mariángeles and her mother," she said with a wink.

I smiled. It was a good dream that she had, a good plan, and I really hoped it would work for her. "Take care of Sara, will you? I am going to miss her. God be with you," I said, and stepping into my sandals, I gave Miranda a last hug and fled as noiselessly as I could, first out of the bamboo patch and then in the direction she had told me to go.

Chapter 12

Illinois, 1960

Laura

It was 1960 and time dragged on, slower than a donkey's pregnancy. Sally got involved with writing for the school newspaper, which left Laura alone for long stretches after school. She began helping out at the school library, shelving books that were returned. This involved removing the small card with the stamped date of when the book was due, from the inside cover of the book, and recording its return in a large notebook where the title had been carefully written. She would lay a ruler over the page and meticulously scroll down through the titles until she found the correct one, the put the date in the "Returned" column and initial it. Afterwards she would stack the book in the small trolley, which she would later wheel to the shelves to file the books.

If the title of a book sounded particularly interesting, she would make a note of it and afterwards, check it out herself and spend the afternoon reading. She would either go to the orchard or down by the pond, as both were places where she would not be bothered. But she could only do this once her farm work was completed. In this manner she read about adventures in far-away lands and began to dream of moving somewhere else where things would be different and much more interesting than they were in Illinois.

At home, Laura and Sally were alternately best friends, whispering about boys or the latest dresses that they saw the city girls wearing, the hats they wished they could buy and curling each other's hair, or they were quarreling about whose turn it was to muck out the barn or clean the ashes from the wood-burning stove.

"Can't I please borrow your red sweater?" Sally begged.

"Yes, but first I need you to pluck my eyebrows," Laura said.

"I don't have time to do that, I'm running late already," Sally said.

"Fine, but then you can't have my sweater."

"You're so mean!" Sally said, coming back into the bathroom and accepting the tweezers. "I should tell Mother that you pluck."

"You wouldn't dare!"

"Hm," said Sally.

"I'll never lend you any of my sweaters again."

"I was just kidding, golly, you don't have to get yourself in a huff, you know," said Sally.

Laura smiled. She sat on a low stool and leaned her head back over the sink so that the bathroom light could shine on her face. It only took a few seconds and she wasn't asking that much, she knew, it's just that Sally loved to banter.

But time still seemed to take forever and the last few weeks before college started, in the fall of 1960, Laura despaired that it would never be time for her to leave the house. Steven had taken over egg collecting, and the family had sold most of the cows, so it didn't take long to milk the last few every morning. After finishing her chores, Laura would head to the library and spend the rest of the day there, either working or sitting between the aisles on the dusty carpeted floor, lost in a good book.

Finally, the day arrived and Laura moved out of her home for good. Sally cried and even Steven got a little red in the nose. Laura's two older brothers drove over from Urbana and helped her take her things to her dorm in the big city.

At the university, she lived in a small all-girls dormitory run by nuns. There were strict curfew times in the evening, but during the day she could come and go as she pleased. She enrolled in first year teaching classes and worked hard to forget her small life of the past. Sally managed to come visit about once a month, and both girls stayed up late into the night talking.

Sally told her about the changes to the farm, which were minimal, but which added up over time. Their father was feeling his age and had contracted out the land to be farmed by some neighbors. Their oldest dog passed away. The pigs that were butchered were not replaced so the passel was decreasing in size.

She also told Laura of the gossip at school. "Betty Higgins came to school wearing a scarf around her neck and her little brother said it was because she had a hickey. Then at lunch, Tommy Badger pulled it off and she had two of them! Her folks found out and she is in big trouble and is grounded until she turns eighteen!"

And Laura told her about her classes and how much she loved learning about teaching. She also told Sally about the boy she was seeing, Tony Shapiro, who was of Italian heritage.

"Is he Catholic? You know Mom and Pop will pitch a fit if you don't marry another Catholic." Laura's parents had not come to visit, but it seemed like they were always there anyway, as subtext to whatever conversation the girls had.

"Yes, of course he's Catholic. All Italians are Catholic," Laura reassured her.

But the next time that Sally came to visit and asked about Tony, Laura told her that they had broken up.

"He was mean to the waiter at the diner when we went out for hamburgers."

Sally looked at her incredulously. "But did he do anything to you?"

"Didn't have to. I've been thinking about it for a long time. I don't want someone like Pop, and I think this is one of the ways to be sure. See how they treat other people. Especially people who they think are not important."

"Like if he's mean to someone else he'll be mean to you?"

"Maybe. Some day. I just can't abide mean people, you know. Had enough with Mom and Pop."

Sally hugged Laura. "You're so wise. You're the best big sister, you know it?"

Laura smiled. "You're not so bad for a little sister either."

Chapter 13

El Salvador, 1960

Sesi

When I left the village of Lourdes that morning after Miranda woke me up in the bamboo patch, I walked along the edge of the road, from one small town to the next. Every time I had a chance, I would ask a kind woman for directions to San Salvador. I walked for a long time, though I can't say how many days because they blurred together and I lost count. But I could tell that I was getting closer over time as people more readily pointed the way, instead of looking at me like I was crazy.

It was hard for me to settle down at first, since I was so determined to reach San Salvador all at once. I would work for a few days or a few weeks in a house, then take my wages and move on. As I trudged along the dusty streets, some of which were paved, I stepped around muddy pot holes, and kept an eye out for any posted signs advertising the need for a *muchacha* or a *niñera*. I walked up and down the rows of houses, peering at windows with my heart pumping heavily in my chest. My heart was always hoping to get lucky, but my time for that had not yet come. There were entire villages in which no one needed help in their houses and I would move on, always finding a place to sleep before nightfall.

My lucky sandals were a bit too big for me—I had very

96

narrow feet so most sandals were too big, even if the length was right. In this case, my sandals were both too wide and too long. I didn't mind, though. I'd had them for several years and since I spent time watching them as I walked, I'll tell you the story of how I got them. I inherited them from the oldest daughter at the place I worked right before going to Sara's house. Her name was Conchi, and she had gone to San Miguel to work as a secretary, and when she moved out, she left them behind. I would not have taken them had it not been that my old sandals had worn all the way through, with ragged holes like eyes for my feet to see right through to the ground. It was like I was walking barefoot when I wore them, only it didn't look as bad as if I had actually gone barefoot, and from the top, you couldn't see the holes anyway. That would have been embarrassing. But it was Camila, Conchi's mother, who took it upon herself to throw my old ones away one night, while I slept. She replaced them with her daughter's sandals.

Thinking of Conchi was helpful because it always reminded me of how lucky I was, which is a good thing when you are determined to walk all the way to San Salvador and you don't know how to get there. What happened to Conchi after she left home is sad. She only worked for a few months in San Miguel before she developed pancreatic troubles. They operated on her and she ended up dying—I guess she lost too much blood or something. Poor thing, I felt sorry for her but I was glad that at least she wasn't a mother herself, leaving behind a little girl or boy to fend for themselves with an angry, drinking father. Conchi was a nice lady and she was missed by all of us in the house.

At first, when I wore her sandals I found myself constantly hoping that it was not a bad omen to be wearing them——that it would not mean I was literally following in her footsteps and would end up dead on the operating table at some point soon. But then I reminded myself that she left them behind.

Maybe that was her mistake. Maybe as long as she had them, she was protected and leaving them was what caused her pancreas to stop working. Of course, I know life doesn't really work that way, and there is no magic, like in the Monkey Princess story, but I still felt better, realizing that now that I had them, I was safe like she used to be.

I am grateful, though, remembering that first of many acts of kindnesses that Camila showed me. There are a lot of gentle people out in the world, and it's been my great fortune to have found so many of them in my travels.

I wish I could have stayed at that house longer. I was very happy there, but it was not meant to be. After Conchi passed away, Camila and her husband kind of folded in on themselves like that little card table the servants at Sara's house used to eat on the back patio. I could understand that sadness, even if I had not experienced it personally. They were despondent and then they got the idea to move back to Metapan, where they were originally from. They offered to take me with them but I wanted to go to San Salvador and Metapan was in the wrong direction. So we parted ways. That's how it goes sometimes, life is like a yo-yo: you have the good fortune of getting sandals with no holes on the bottom, and of not getting pancreatic problems and dying on the operating table, but the misfortune of no longer having employment and a kind family for whom to work. But then my luck got good and I went to work at Sara's house, which was really great. Until my luck ran out again and here I was, watching my toes contract with each step to keep from losing my sandals.

The sound made by the slapping of my sandals as I walked on, hoping my luck would improve soon, reminded me of a drum, beating out a tune. If I had known how to whistle, there are many times that I would have considered doing it as I walked, even though it's not appropriate for women to whistle. It was ironic that I had that thought because the next job that I got was working with another child, a little boy, who could whistle like no one I've ever met before or since. He was generally a quiet child, didn't speak much, but when the mood hit him, like when he was taking a bath or playing with his toys, he would whistle as though he had the soul of a little bird. His name was Gustavo and I liked minding him.

Gustavo was about four years old when I went to work at his house, a few weeks after I had left Sara's house. I have to tell you a funny story that happened when I was working there. One day, a chicken flew over the high, cement wall between the houses and landed in the patio where Gustavo was playing. He was so excited to see this chicken come down from heaven that he chased her around. Poor thing, she was squawking and shedding feathers as she scrambled to get away. I don't know why she didn't just fly back to where she had come from, but she didn't. I saw what was going on and went to catch the chicken too, and soon the two of us had scared the bird into a corner and as she jumped up, I caught her.

Gustavo pulled on my dress as he struggled to take her away from me, but I was afraid he would hurt her, or get hurt, so I put the chicken into a cloth bag and took her back to the neighbor's house. Gustavo cried for what seemed like a year but must have been just two days and when I saw the neighbor's maid, Carmen, on the way to the market the next morning, I told her how upset Gustavo was.

Two weeks later there was a knock on the front door. The neighbor had brought a basket with a gift for Gustavo. I took the basket to him. It had a white cloth dotted with little yellow flowers over the top of the basket, and you could see that something was alive inside. I urged him to gently lift the cover and he peeked inside. There were five little baby chickens, all yellow and fluffy and squirming around, climbing over each other and saying "*pio, pio, pio*," the way baby chicks do.

They were adorable. But they ended up having miserable, short lives. When Gustavo's father asked him, late that afternoon, where the chickens were, he reached into his trouser pockets and pulled them out, one at a time. Poor little things, their legs were all broken by the next morning. Gustavo's mother, *Doña* Hilda, stepped in and sequestered the little chicks and put them in a shoe box with cotton lining the bottom. She got toothpicks and thread and made little casts for the bird legs to grow stronger. I know because it was my job to change out the pooped-on cotton each morning and put fresh cotton and shredded newspaper down for them.

But Gustavo's one obsession was to get at those little birds and he always found a way to reach them, even when I put the box on top of the refrigerator. He wasn't a bad kid. He was just four years old and he wanted to have those birds as a toy.

One morning when I got back from the market, *Doña* Hilda told me that she had found Gustavo standing in the patio, six paces from the wall. He had gotten down the shoe box with chickens in it and as she watched, he picked up a chicken and lobbed it at the wall.

"I screamed at him, Sesi, when I saw what he was doing," she told me.

"But, why was he...?" I asked.

Just then Gustavo came in the room, his nose still red from crying.

"Tell Sesi why you were throwing the chickens at the wall," *Doña* Hilda asked of her son.

At first he crossed his arms and mutely refused to speak. But I cajoled him, promising to tell him a story later on if he told me. Finally, he broke down and said, "I was teaching them how to fly."

I covered my mouth with my hand so he would not see

100

my smile and turned away from him.

That evening the little chicks began giving up their lives, and by morning, every one of them was lying on their side, eyes open wide and unmoving, their toothpick wrapped legs sticking out at odd angles from their fuzzy yellow bodies. We buried them in the patio, by the eucalyptus tree, and Gustavo cried for another two days.

Two weeks after that incident, Gustavo's godmother, a very nice woman who was very heavy set and wore long skirts that went almost down to her ankles, brought Gustavo a present. It was a *perico*, a little green bird, that he named Chico. Many people kept these birds as pets. They would catch them from the wild, raiding the parents' nest, and then raise them from the time they were little. They kept their wings trimmed so they couldn't fly away.

This little Chico was the cutest thing I'd ever seen, with a small yellow ring around each of his big, black eyes, and a red patch on his neck, like he was wearing a bandana. He took to Gustavo immediately. We had to clip Chico's wings every three weeks to keep him from flying away, but other than that, the bird took care of himself. We kept him in a cage for a few days when we first got him, but Gustavo climbed on the cage and the wire frame bent and the bird was freed from its jail. After that, Gustavo walked around with the bird on his head all day long, and although *Doña* Hilda was afraid the bird would poop on her son's head, he never did.

I stayed at Gustavo's house well into 1962, until I had to quit. I really hated to leave there, but sometimes people just keep asking you to do more, and more until it gets to be too much. What happened is that their other maid had quit, so instead of replacing her, they gave me all of her work. It was slow at first, and like I said, I really liked Gustavo and *Doña* Hilda, but over time they asked me to start doing all of the washing, which left my hands red and sore, and all of the ironing and then the cooking and shopping. Since they expected me to mind Gustavo while he was awake during the day, that meant that I had a lot left to do once he went to sleep at night. It was a small family I guess they thought that since I was young I would just do it all and not complain. I did do it all for a few weeks, but then I realized that the situation was never going to get better so I snuck out one night and never returned.

Chapter 14

Illinois, 1961-1962

Laura

Laura's first year in college came and went in a flash, and soon it was the fall of 1961 and she was a sophomore at the university, making good grades, but money was always so tight that she was not happy.

"You should apply for a job," Sally suggested.

It wasn't that she hadn't thought of that, it was just that she didn't know where to begin looking. Her only experience had been in the library and there were no jobs available there. Then one day she passed by a bakery. The smell was absolutely heavenly and she looked up to the sign, in spite of the fact that she knew that she could not afford to buy anything inside. It was called Laura's Pastry Shop. And there was a "Help Wanted" sign in the window. A miracle. Laura marched right in and applied.

"What're your credentials, sweetheart?" said the elder Laura, a big, buxomly woman with impossibly orange hair and a bright smile.

"I've been cooking since I was this tall," said Laura. "I grew up on a farm and I can make any kind of pie there is." It was a bold claim, but as she said it, Laura felt confident that it was true.

103

Older Laura ran her eyes up and down the young woman standing perfectly straight in front of her. As she did so, her long eyelashes waved like small feathery hand-held fans that were cooling her face.

"Are you a hard worker?"

"I am."

"And a good learner?"

"I'm in my second year at college, and my grades are good."

"What's the most important thing about making a pie crust?"

Laura smiled. This was a lesson she had learned when she was eleven years old. "You can't knead it or touch it too much. As soon as you add the ice water to the flour and lard, you clump it into a ball and then roll it out, straight away."

Older Laura raised a blonde eyebrow. "Well then, I reckon you'll do," she said. She had taken an instant liking to Laura junior and soon the two were making pies, being careful to add a tablespoon of lemon juice to the apples, or cinnamon rolls (with a touch of nutmeg) or sugar cookies with just the right amount of cream of tartar.

Laura loved working at the bakery and in many ways, Laura senior was like the mother she had never had.

"You're not still fretting over that B you got on your last test in Psychology?" Laura senior would say affectionately. "You'll do better next time."

And whenever Laura junior had a date, Laura senior wanted to hear all about it. "Don't spare any details, kiddo," she would say.

Laura junior did not always comply, but she also did not have a very active dating life as she seemed to have standards that were too high for the boys who asked her out. Word got out that she was hard to please and the number of fellows asking her out dropped from few to practically none. But Laura was busy studying and she found all of the emotional support she could have wished for at the bakery.

Laura senior's easy affection and friendliness was a real gift to Laura junior and it made her feel grounded and secure in a way she had never experienced at home. As she reflected on the older woman's kindness, one day when she was walking home, Laura junior made the decision that she would be this kind of mother and friend when she had children.

Laura finished her second year of college in May of 1962 and again she stayed on campus for the summer, working full-time at the bakery since classes were not in session. With the money she made and a small scholarship that she won, she was able to pay her way through the schoolyear.

On Saturday afternoons, when Laura finished her work at the bakery, she often went to the movie theater with her two closest friends, Dottie and Millie. They would spend the entire afternoon there since a single pass allowed each of them to watch the same movie over and over again, up to four times.

One Saturday in October of 1962, the three friends watched Lawrence of Arabia with Peter O'Toole. The combination of the wide sprawling desert on the big screen, Peter O'Toole's chiseled features and the dark, handsome foreigners enthralled Laura. When the movie was finished, she decided to stay and watch it again. Her friends left after the first showing—Dottie's parents were coming into town and Millie had to study for a big test on Monday. Laura didn't mind staying by herself as she often watched the movie a second time to sink into the story again and imagine herself as one of the characters, swept away by the handsome stranger.

Half way through the second showing, Laura noticed a

man sit down next to her. She didn't know who he was. He had entered when the theater was already dark, and had brought a huge pail of popcorn.

"You like some?" he asked in an accented whisper.

Normally Laura didn't speak to strange men. Her first instinct was to look around for Millie and Dottie, but she remembered that they had left. She was alone. She toyed briefly with the idea of getting up and leaving but the movie was terrific and her stomach growled at the smell of the warm, buttery goodness that he was offering her. She and her friends never bought popcorn—they could not afford such a luxury.

She peered up at the face of her new companion and was immediately smitten by his handsome features. She liked his exotic aquiline nose, his jet-black eyebrows and his curly hair. It was as if he had stepped off of the silver screen to come to sit with her.

No one she knew had hair that rich ebony color. Her own hair had been so pale when she was little that it was almost hard to see that she had any hair at all. His eyes were the color of the hot chocolate served on hayrides in late October, after the corn crops had been picked and the ground shimmered with hard frost. And his skin was a lovely tan, not pale, like hers, but as dark as a chestnut tree in the fall.

"Golly, thanks," she said and they talked, whispering between scenes as the movie played. When it finished, they stayed in their seats and watched it again. He was also a student, on a visa, and this was his fourth year, although he had also attended college in his own country prior to moving here, so he was actually three years older than she was. When he first told her that he was from El Salvador, Laura smiled politely. She had heard of it but she would have been hard-pressed to locate it on an unlabeled map.

Laura and her new friend agreed to meet for dinner the

following weekend and he walked her back to her dorm, planting a small kiss on each of her blushing cheeks before he bade her goodnight. Laura got no sleep that night, reliving each and every part of their conversation multiple times, looking for hidden meaning in his words. He was not like any of the boys she had ever dated. And, as far as she could remember, she had never felt as excited about any of them as she felt now, having spent an afternoon with Rodrigo. Rodrigo Manuel. Even the name was titillating. She couldn't remember his last name—something completely unpronounceable that started with an "A" and sounded mysterious and appealing in equal parts.

The next day Laura went to the library and leafed through a large blue atlas with glossy pages. As soon as she saw how far away the small Latin American country was from Illinois, she felt that it was meant to be. Her prince had come to sweep her off her feet and take her to his kingdom in a land where she would live in a jungle village, monkeys vying for her attention and lovely flowers everywhere she looked.

Well, he hadn't mentioned the kingdom part, or the monkeys, or even the jungle, and she wasn't all the way swept off her feet yet, but dreaming was free. She scanned the card catalog for books about El Salvador, then checked them out and walked home with her arms full.

That night she read about the history of the tiny country, going all the way back to the time of the Indians. She was fascinated and had never realized that relatives of the Aztecs had lived all the way down there, building pyramids and doing complicated math. She saw the beautiful pictures of volcanoes and dense green jungles and many colorful fruits and wanted to see and taste them all.

At work in the bakery, Laura senior noticed Laura junior's mood as she was kneading the bread.

"You look particularly happy. Wait, don't tell me!

You've gone and got yourself a boyfriend?" she asked, pausing to sprinkle a cloud of flour onto the smooth, warm surface of the spongy dough.

Laura gave her a hug and told her about the movie encounter.

"Sounds sweet," Laura senior said, "What's he look like? Blonde hair and gorgeous blue eyes?"

Laura junior had purposefully not mentioned anything about Rodrigo's looks as she had guessed that Laura senior would not take kindly to a foreigner. And she was right. As soon as she described Rodrigo, the older woman was instantly on her guard.

"Them foreigners, you gotta be careful with them, Laura. They only want one thing and that's a piece of a white girl's you-know-what. I suspect he's probably just playing with you, then he'll go home and marry one of his own kind, like as not."

Laura nodded solemnly and teared up. Even though she had anticipated the woman's words, they stung her.

"Aw, honey, there I went and made you cry!" said Laura senior, dusting off her hands and reaching out to give the younger Laura a hug. "I'm sorry! There, there. You're not to blame, sweetheart, there's no way you could have known that. It's not your fault!"

"But he was so nice to me. We talked for hours."

Laura senior shook her head. "Poor, sweet little Laura. You're so innocent, breaks my heart. But let me tell you, best thing you can do is stay far away from them foreigners. You'll forget about him soon, too, don't you worry. Have I told you about my friend Lilly's son, he's in the navy, and a right good man he is too. I'll get you set up with him as soon as he gets back."

Laura junior mulled over her friend's words the rest of

the afternoon. She knew that her own parents—and her Aunt Susie and Uncle Bill, Jimmy's parents, would feel the same way. And, for all she knew, they could be right. After all, what did she know about Rodrigo? She had met him only once. He could be leading her on. He could be trying to seduce her.

She tightened her jaw and bravely made the decision to cancel her upcoming date with Rodrigo. It would be better this way, before it progressed any farther.

But her heart was having a civil war with her mind. Her chest hurt and it was hard for her to swallow. Even her arms and legs felt torpid as they fought against her brain's decision. She was feeling angry and irritated by the time she got back to the dorm that evening. That's when she saw that there was a big bouquet of a dozen red roses set in hills of fragrant baby's breath and edged with perfectly shaped pine-green ferns. Taped to the vase was a card on which Rodrigo had written in bold, handsome strokes, "Counting the hours until our dinner. Yours, Rodrigo."

She considered the note for several minutes, her heart pounding like a grandfather clock in a tiny room, and decided that she would go out to dinner with him after all. She would only agree to one date and then she would see what happened. But the decision seemed to release the spell on her body and suddenly she felt light and easy. Her arms and legs were working again and she could have danced for hours. Surely that meant something, she reasoned. Surely that meant that she had seen something in Rodrigo that Laura senior (and her family) could not know.

Laura's friends were ambivalent when they met him on Friday night. Rodrigo was tall and handsome, they agreed. But they had reservations.

"A bit old, wouldn't you say? And isn't his skin too dark?" her friends helpfully pointed out when they whisked her off to powder her nose before her date.

Laura crossed her arms. "You haven't even given him a chance. You just took one look at him and made the decision."

"But, so did you," said Molly. "We left you at the end of the movie and a few hours later you come home with a date. That's a fast decision."

"Look, Laura, we're just telling you because we care so much about you. Can't you see?" said Dottie, taking Laura's hand in her own. "He's too foreign for these parts. And what kind of a name is Rodrigo, anyway? Better if his name was Bill or Chuck. Your parents will have a cow if they find out you are dating him."

Laura released Dottie's hand.

"Fine, but don't say we didn't warn you," said Dottie as Laura went back out to meet Rodrigo.

"Everything all right?" asked Rodrigo when she returned, her face red.

Laura positioned a smile on her face. "Fine."

"I've waited all week to see you. I can wait a bit longer if you need more time."

Laura looked up into his warm, brown eyes and felt her heart softening. "No, it's really fine. Let's go."

Rodrigo beamed and helped her with her coat. Then he rushed ahead to open the door for her and gave her his arm to hold as they walked. Laura had forgotten her gloves, so she nestled her hand in the crook of his arm and stuffed her other hand in her pocket.

"You are cold," he said, looking down at her and pulling his arm closer to his body, drawing her closer. "Would you like my coat?"

"No, I'm fine," said Laura, smiling now. No one had ever offered her his coat.

"It is not very far," he said. "I hope you will like the restaurant I have chosen."

"I'm sure I will," she said, beginning to feel warmer with the brisk pace.

Over dinner they found lots to talk about. He was from the city, so their childhoods had been very different. He told her of his father, who had died when he was in high school, and of how much he had missed him over the years. She told him about Sally and about hunting trips with Jimmy.

"So I better not ever make you angry," he said with a twinkle in his eye. "Or you might get your gun and shoot me."

Laura laughed. "That's right," she said.

The dinner flew by and after that they went dancing. Laura didn't have much experience, but Rodrigo was well-schooled and led her confidently through the steps, placing one hand on the small of her back and holding one of her hands firmly with his other hand. She had more fun than she had ever had on a date.

When she got back to the dorm, her friends were waiting to pepper her with questions. "How was it? Did he kiss you? Did he try anything?"

She told them the highlights of the date and they softened. "He sounds much nicer than I would have expected," they agreed. "Still, he's so different from everyone around here."

But it was precisely the fact that he was so different that had attracted Laura. She still wanted to get away from her life on the farm, and in Illinois, and what better way than to marry someone from south of the border?

After a few more dates with Rodrigo, during which he continued to shower her with attention and kindness, she made the decision and fell whole-heartedly in love with him. They went to movies, always walking in at the midway point and

111

staying to watch the beginning afterwards, but only if they liked the ending. They took long walks in the park along the lake, watching the trees turn brilliant colors before the harsh autumnal winds blew away their leaves. The ate dinner and went dancing. They studied together for exams. It was the best time of her whole life.

Chapter 15

Illinois, 1962

Laura

"In my home country, there is no autumn and the trees are never bare," said Rodrigo. Their courtship was now going strong and winter was settling over Chicago. But it was the holiday season and there were multi-colored lights and carols and bright silver bells on lamp posts. It was a lovely time of year.

"You mean you never get to kick up piles of leaves and rake them into huge mounds so you could jump into them?" she said, realizing for the first time how fond she was of the fall.

"Oh, the trees do lose their leaves. But they do it throughout the year, little by little—no fuss. But you can walk through the tropical forest and crunch the leaves."

"But the colorful show?"

"No, but we do have many plants whose red or yellow leaves are there all year."

"And spring?"

Rodrigo shook his head. "But we have beautiful flowers all year long, many of which cannot grow in the parks here. Orchids, bougainvilleas, and many more whose names I don't

113

know in English."

Laura paused, trying to imagine a world where there were only two seasons, rainy and dry. Although she could accept it intellectually, having never really travelled farther than a hundred miles from where she was born made it really challenging to picture that other world where the clouds, the winds and the sun behaved so differently from what she had always known.

When the weather got too cold Laura and Rodrigo took shorter walks and then went back to his apartment for big mugs of hot chocolate. They talked about books they loved and Rodrigo showed her some poetry that he had written.

"It sounds much better in Spanish," he assured her.

Laura marveled at his ability to create art out of words and decided that she would learn Spanish. Someday.

"An civil engineer who writes poetry," Sally said, when she came up for a visit. "Golly, Sis, that's so nice!" She and Rodrigo hit it off well, though she agreed with Laura that her parents would probably not welcome Rodrigo into their home.

Soon it was Christmas and Rodrigo went home to El Salvador. "My mother does not live in the capital city and I may not see much of her, but I have close friends from high school and my first years of college in San Salvador. My friend Adelmo is like a brother to me. And he is getting married to his sweetheart, Adelgonda. I cannot miss this wedding. Won't you come with me?"

As much as she would have loved to go with him, Laura was not ready for such a big commitment yet. She was not sure if she would have gone with him to a wedding in Indiana, let alone in another country. And besides, she didn't have a passport.

"You must get a passport, my dearest. I will want to take you to my beautiful country at some point in the future," he said, and then kissed her goodbye and walked down the small tunnel to board the airplane. She watched him go with a heavy heart, her lips still tingling from the kiss.

The future. He was talking about her and him, together in the future. Laura said goodbye and spent many happy afternoons replaying his words in her mind. She was thoroughly and happily in love.

Now she faced three weeks without him. Should she stay in Chicago, or return home for the holidays? She really didn't want to go back. She had visited the farm for a brief week over the summer, and although she no longer had to carry her shotgun around to ward off her father, things were not the same. Sally was never around—she was always doing something with the newspaper. And Steven spent hours at Jimmy's house, hunting with their younger cousin, Mike.

Laura's mother was cold and distant, as she had been in Laura's youth, but now it was almost more intolerable and Laura had spent the better part of her days up in her room, reading old books and sorting through a box of mementos from her youth.

"In case you're wondering, I could sure use the extra help if you're thinking of staying up here in the Windy City over the holidays," said the older Laura at work that afternoon.

Laura looked up at her gratefully. "Yeah, I was planning on staying," she said, even though she had only made up her mind that minute to stay.

That afternoon she gathered her change and went to call her parents. "I'm really sorry, but Ms. Laura really needs me at the bakery, and plus, I've got a lot to do. And there's so much snow on the roads, the busses might not be safe, or reliable," she said to her mother.

"Well, it don't much matter anyway," her mother said. "Your pop is getting too arthritic to cut much wood so we'll

115

probably just set up some beds and sleep in kitchen, by the hearth. Wouldn't want you catching yourself to death a cold if you come by and stay here. You stay there and help out Ms. Laura and get your studying done."

It was probably the nicest thing her mother had ever said to her and Laura felt tears pricking her eyes. She stayed on in the dorm, and later said goodbye to Dottie and Molly as well. They were growing apart, since Laura spent so much time with Rodrigo and they still thought that she was making a mistake by dating him.

When she wasn't working at the bakery, making all sorts of pudding and Christmas breads and rolls for the hundreds of customers who had put in special orders, Laura used the time to catch up on her reading and class preparation. She also spent hours sitting in the library, which was warmer than the dorm room, writing Rodrigo long letters in which she recounted everything that happened in her day, in excruciating detail. It was as if she was having one long conversation with him, sharing all of her thoughts in a stream of consciousness manner. And of course, she sprinkled kisses and love on every page.

Chapter 16

El Salvador, 1962
Sesi

I'm not proud of leaving Gustavo's house the way I did, sneaking off in the night. I know I should have said goodbye, especially since I had been there for several years, but I just didn't want to face their sadness and disappointment. Still, it was wrong and fate punished me for being a coward like that.

Afterwards, there seemed to be no more *niñera* jobs to be had so I worked as a *muchacha*, a job which involves a lot of water and soap and sore hands. I spent time scrubbing floors and fetid toilets, washing dishes, washing clothes, and wiping windows with newspapers that left my arms black and sooty.

Some jobs were better than others, and occasionally I had the good fortune of hearing about a new job before I quit the old one. Sometimes the new job took me in a backwards direction, to a village that lay in the opposite direction to San Salvador, so it was like walking with one leg shorter than the other and going in slow circles through the forest. But in general, I kept making my way toward the capital.

Once, I had the great good fortune to run into Miranda. This was on a day when I realized that I had accidentally walked into a village that was in the wrong direction. I was just about to turn around and leave the village again, without even inquiring about work, when I saw her. She had lost some weight and was

117

wearing a different dress from either of the two I used to know. I recognized her first by the scars on her face. She had not seen me so I approached her as soon as she finished buying some mangoes and *jocotes* from a vendor in the market.

When she realized who I was her face lit up like bright fire on a dark night and she hugged me tight. Then we both laughed and cried at the coincidence of seeing each other again, something that I had never dreamed would happen. She told me that she had quit working at Sara's house too, about eight months after I left. Apparently the good-luck charm of her scars stopped having their effect on *Don* Enrique and when she saw that he was getting too interested in getting some alone-time with her, she quickly got out of there.

"But, how are you, Sesi?" she asked over and over, and then before I could answer she would make some remark about my appearance or start telling me about something that had occurred while she still worked at Sara's house.

"You're taller now, Sesi, I can't believe you grew another five centimeters! How are you? But you wouldn't believe how much Sara cried when she found out that you had left. I think she cried for a whole month. It was so bad that even *Doña* Fabiola agreed that we should take you back and sent *Don* Enrique out to find you. I prayed that he would not find you of course, because *Don* Enrique was the same as ever and the old lady just kept getting crazier as time passed by. Did you hear what she did to me right before I left?"

Of course, there was no way I could have heard anything about the goings-on in that household as it had been many months since I had worked there and I'd not seen anyone whom I'd known when I had lived there.

Miranda made a loud clucking sound with her tongue and went on to educate me. "After you left, *Doña* Fabiola took to drinking like an anteater takes to the forest. She was drunk nearly every day and her mind went even farther downhill after that. One day she came into the kitchen when I had gone to the back patio to hang up some dish towels. Just as I walked back in I saw her pouring the last of a quart of liquor into the stew I had made for dinner. She ruined it! And right before I was ready to serve it. Can you believe it?"

I went as still as a boulder from the shock. *Doña* Fabiola did drink a lot, but I had never seen her acting so crazy like that.

"What did you do with the food?" I asked, hardly daring to imagine the situation.

"I served it, of course. Not to Sara, she's such a picky eater, that one, still as she was when you were there," she said. I smiled inwardly, remembering, with more fondness than I might have imagined that I would, my struggles trying to get her to take a few bites of food.

"And when *Don* Enrique took a big spoonful of it, he grimaced and promptly spit it out all over the tablecloth!"

We laughed softly and shook our hands, making our fingers slap together.

"You know, Sesi, it took me a long time after you left to realize that I was wasting my time staying in that same house. I'm so glad that I left. I might have even followed in your footsteps as I left the village of Lourdes, who knows? It took me three whole days to get to this village and here I am now. I got a job as a cook at a house here and things are going well for me. But you! Just seeing you is good for my soul," she said, smiling at me affectionately. "How are things for you?"

"Things are okay," I said, and then I told her that I had been working at Gustavo's house but I had just left there and was looking for another job.

"You should come work at the house with me! Let me talk to the woman I work for."

It was a tempting offer and my spoiled stomach immediately growled its approval, but I managed to remain in control and shook my head.

"You don't want to work at the same place as me?"

"It's not that," I said, taking her hand. "It's that I need to keep making my way to San Salvador. I was going to apply in the next village down that way, I said pointing, or the one after that. If I don't keep going, I'm never going to make it there."

"Are you still trying to find a house that pays a lot, like Linda?" she asked.

This made me smile, to think that she still remembered the story I told her about my mother's neighbors daughter. I nodded.

"Well, then," she said and hugged me once more and said, "Good luck and Godspeed, my dear Sesi. And now I had better get back before I'm missed. But if you're ever back in town, send a message and I'll come out to meet you. We can have a nice chat, so just send word and I'll find a way to go meet you, promise?"

"I will," I said, swallowing hard to keep tears from flooding my eyes as I said goodbye. I watched her walk away and I felt like a little piece of my chest was breaking off and going with her. Seeing her had also reminded me of my sweet Sara, and the pain of missing her came back too.

When Miranda had walked for several hundred paces, she turned the corner and I could no longer see her. Then I turned around too, and headed down the road, toward the next village. As I walked, I looked down at my feet. I could see my long, skinny toes curved like a bird's talons over the front edge of the sandals, as if they are peeking over a cliff, trying to decide if they should dive off. Meanwhile, the back of each sandal dragged, making that clapping noise I told you about earlier.

Clap, step, clap, step.

I wondered how long it would be before I got to San Salvador. Everyone said there was sure to be lots of work there. I also thought of Linda, the daughter of my mother's neighbor, who sent home much more money than I did. The last time that I had seen my mother, she had reminded me of this and I had promised to get to San Salvador as soon as I could.

The good thing was that when I was between jobs and near the countryside, I was never hungry. There were mangos everywhere: sour green ones which were crunchy and hard as apples, or soft orange ones, juicy in my hands. There were *nances*, sweet yellow fruits the size of grapes, *mamee* apples, which, when ripe, were creamy and delicious. If I was really lucky, I'd find some long brown *caraos*, with their tangy, sticky dark pulp which I would chew off the seeds. Often there were also tart red and orange *marañones* whose seeds I would add to the contents of my plastic bag, saving them to roast for cashew nuts. There were also sour yellow and orange *jocotes* that left my mouth all puckered, bananas, and even coconuts or avocados if I was really desperate. Coconuts were mostly considered dog food, but I found them quite nice when I was good and hungry.

The memories of these fruits made my tummy rumble jealously. The city was different. In small cities there was no problem as I could still escape into the countryside when I was hungry, but larger ones required skill. For one thing, people were always trying to steal from me. I kept my *colones* tucked into my bosom and only had one or two in my pocket at any given time, ready to use when it was time to pay. But sometimes people tried to steal more subtly, by charging me double the price for a *pupusa*. I lost money a few times when I first set out from Sara's house, before I learned how to haggle and now I did quite well for myself.

Still, as I searched, looking at houses up and down the

121

gravel streets, straining to read any signs that might be posted, it was disheartening to see that yet again, no one needed a maid. Hot and sweaty, I trudged to the center of town and saw a park with a fountain in the middle. It was two-tiered, with a statue of the Virgin in the center. Her arms were extended to either side and cool water flowed from her delicate fingers into the smaller upper bowl and then spilled into the wider lower bowl. Each of the bowls were scalloped and inset with bright teal-colored ceramic tiles. The square tiles were small, like the ones used in bathrooms, but out here in the sun they sparkled beautifully.

I knew that soon I would need to hunt for a safe place to spend the night—a thicket of trees, a small shed—somewhere where I could hide and sleep. I hated being out after dark as danger, even in small towns like this, increased at night. And even when I did manage to finally nod off, it was always a light sleep in case any stray dogs would come around to find me. I was terrified of dogs, especially after hearing how they howled the night I spent in the bamboo clump when I left Sara's house.

I went up to the fountain and, leaning over the edge, I took a long drink from the water that fell like a small river. Then I splashed some of the cool goodness on my face and neck. The town hall clock struck 4:00 pm, and I knew that by 6:00 pm it would be dark. I was very close to San Salvador by now, which meant that this place was more perilous than the towns I had been in before and it might take some time to find a safe place to spend the night.

Since I only had two hours I decided that I would walk down the last street, where there were some nicer looking houses, and knock on a few doors to see if anyone needed work, and then call it a day. Dipping my hand once more into the fountain, I swished the pretty green algae to one side and then cupped a bit of water which I dragged over my hair, making it flatten down. I looked at my wobbly reflection. There, that was better.

I shook the excess water off my hands and ran them up and down my skirt to dry them. Then I picked up my plastic bag with my belongings, and headed toward the last road. The houses were definitely nicer there. I was a bit nervous so I took a deep breath to get up some courage before I knocked at the first door. I waited patiently, but no one answered. I went to the second house. Here an old lady, clearly a servant, came to the door. It was one of those two part doors, so she opened the top half and kept the bottom part firmly shut. She peered out with myopic eyes embedded in a nest of wrinkled skin, her open mouth harboring just one yellowed tooth.

At first she didn't see me. I guess she was expecting someone taller. When I greeted her she told me they had already received their tortillas for the day, thank you. She was about to shut the top half of the door but I raised my voice and asked her if she knew anyone looking for a cook. She pursed her lips, folding them into even more wrinkles than before, and narrowed her eyes at me. Then she spoke as if talking about me to someone else.

"Well, she's a right little runt of a thing there, isn't she? Not much bigger than a cigarette, wouldn't you say?" she asked of no one in particular. "A cook, eh? Well, you might try asking at the doctor's house. I'm not sure if they need anyone at the moment, but it's always worth asking there. What? You don't know where the doctor's house is? Look at that! She doesn't know where the doctor's house is. Why, it's right where it's always been, four houses down and on the other side of the street."

I thanked her, said a quick but heartfelt prayer to the Virgin Mary to help me find work there if it was meant to be, and walked across the street to the indicated house. The whole way there I walked slowly, nervously rehearsing what I would say when they answered the door. After knocking three separate times I felt my shoulders slump as I turned away. No one was home. And it was getting late. I had to find a place to sleep, so that left me no choice but to return to the doctor's house the next day.

I walked a few blocks back toward the more commercial area of town, and involuntarily followed my nose to the place where they were selling *pupusas*. As my stomach became aware of the rich smell of the melted cheese surrounded by hot corn tortillas, it protested loudly and I remembered that I had eaten only one tortilla and some fruit in the entire day.

But I did not know how far I would have to walk tomorrow if the doctor did not know of anyone looking for a maid, nor did I know how long I would be without work, so I did not want to spend much money. I ordered a single *pupusa*. Then I sat on the bright red bench outside the little shop to eat it. I wanted to gobble the whole thing down immediately, but I forced myself to take small bites, chewing completely. It was hot and fresh and I immediately felt stronger and more clear-headed after eating.

When I finished eating I inspected the little rattan plate, lined with a piece of tissue paper that had grown almost completely transparent from the oil that had leaked from the cheese. I was disappointed to see that no crumbs had escaped my notice.

I had been hungry before, as I've told you, but it seemed that my stomach always forgot how to be hungry. I would find steady employment, get regular meals for weeks or months at a time, and then my stomach would quickly forget how to endure the times of less food. I remember wishing, as Sara had all those years ago, for a pill to quiet my hunger. Maybe the pill would be cheap, and perhaps it would be insipid, but what did that matter if I could then stop worrying about food and get on with things?

I could see now that my stomach was acting like a spoiled child, always demanding what it obviously could not easily have. I scolded it ruthlessly for wanting more, and this reminded me of a story Miranda liked to tell. It was kind of a joke, and it was pretty stupid, if you thought about it, but spending time thinking about it had the desired effect of calming my tummy, so indulge me, if you will.

The story goes that there was a man who was so poor and so hungry, that all he could afford to buy was a single banana. So he went to the fruit stand and bought the largest, prettiest banana, but it was still very small compared to how hungry he was. He was very, very hungry, so he decided it would be better if he ate the banana peel first, and saved the inside for dessert. The peeling was bitter and stringy and it turned his tongue black. Still, he was hungry so he forced himself to eat the entire thing, right down to the woody stalk, which he chewed on for several minutes before managing to swallow it. Once he had finally finished with the peeling, he found that he was no longer hungry, so he threw the banana away.

I found the story to be both ridiculous and fascinating at the same time. Imagine throwing away the banana, I said to myself. Imagine. I must be very careful never to do that.

The next morning I went back to the doctor's house. I knocked and someone answered, but they soon dispatched me, saying that they didn't know of anyone in the area who needed a cook or a *muchacha*.

As I sat despondently by the fountain, trying to figure out where I should go next, I saw a newspaper rolled up and held fast by a rubber band. Someone must have dropped it. I picked it up and after flipping through a few of the pages, I found the classified section. I scanned through the ads, hoping to see something useful. I was pretty sure there would be nothing there for a *muchacha*, and as I went down the columns, my fears were confirmed. There were absolutely no posts at all for people wanting help in their houses.

"You can read, can you, little cigy?" asked the old woman from the night before. I had been concentrating so hard that I had not heard her approaching.

I closed the newspaper hurriedly and looked into her broad, wrinkled face as she towered over me. She had seemed so hard of sight the night before that I was surprised that she even recognized me.

"Yes, ma'am," I said, the blood rising to my face.

"Then I expect she won't do poorly after all, will she?" she said, talking to that invisible person again. "Have you considered working in the capital city?"

I told her that I had and that I was actually making my way there.

"Well, she's nearly there now, isn't she? I reckon she is. You see that over there?" she said, motioning toward the east with her extended lips and a cock of her head.

I looked and I could see the houses of the neighboring village, scattered over the hill.

"That's Santa Tecla. It's the next-door neighbor of San Salvador. Go to Colonia Quezaltepec, and find the cross streets of Calle San Salvador and Avenida 2. Head north from that corner, and go to number 11, a white house with a blue door. There are two red hibiscus bushes next to the front window. *Don* Germán and his wife live there. They are looking for a cook and they want someone who can read."

And that's how my luck changed, finally, for the better, although there was a really bad patch that waited for me as well.

Chapter 17

Illinois, January 1963

Laura

Laura arrived at the airport two hours before Rodrigo's flight was due to land. It was a silly thing to do but she was worried that the bus might be late or get caught in traffic or even have an accident, and any of these events would mean missing him as he emerged from the little hallway that connected to the airplane door. The nearly three weeks of his absence had seemed interminably long and she might as well wait at the airport as anywhere else.

She brought a library book to read, but it sat heavily in her lap as she constantly put it down to observe the people walking by and wonder about their lives. There were the stewardesses in their tight skirts, the black line of their pantyhose making its way neatly up the backs of their legs as they walked. And then came the pilots and co-pilots, in their smart uniforms, their blonde hair combed neatly under their important caps.

There were businessmen with rectangular leather briefcases, their hair slicked back and a determined look in their eyes as they walked briskly to meet an important client. And stopping to make a call on a payphone, she saw a well-dressed woman with shiny red nail polish adorning the tips of her long fingers, carrying a suitcase that had to be a typewriter. Was she a

127

secretary? A famous writer?

Grandmothers and grandfathers arrived at the gates to say goodbye to their adult children and grandchildren who were returning to wherever they lived when it was not the holiday season. She saw the hugs and moist faces of young women as they kissed their white-haired parents and promised they would visit again soon, while their children hopped up and down, full of energy and oblivious to the drama. For an instant, Laura tried to imagine herself saying goodbye like that to her mother. But no, she would never shed tears of sadness over her own departure, nor could she imagine her parents bothering to escort her to the airport, or even the bus station. Then she imagined herself as the elderly woman, bidding adieu to her daughter and grandchildren, and that seemed much more plausible.

Off to the left, a group of young men, all dressed alike in black slacks and blue cardigans over white, collared shirts, jostled each other as they made their way down the hall.

Finally, the black slatted time-table flipped to reveal that Rodrigo's flight was landing. She stood up and went to wait by the exit of the little, dark hallway and eagerly scanned each man's face as he emerged. There were quite a few dark-skinned people, more than she had ever seen together, and for a moment she panicked and wondered if she would recognize him. What if he got a radically different haircut? Or he was behind another person and didn't see her and walked right by and out before she could get his attention?

But then, there he was, carrying a huge bouquet of flowers. It was such a large and gorgeous arrangement that she blushed when she realized he had brought them for her.

"I've missed you, my darling," he said, hugging her and picking her up off the ground for a moment in his embrace. His clean smell of sandalwood filled her nostrils and suffused her with warmth.

"Did you get all my letters?" Laura asked brightly.

"No," he said, "but here are my letters to you." He produced a leather pouch, engraved with the words El Salvador. Also engraved on the cover were a picture of a volcano and a woman walking with a large, shallow basket balanced on her head. Inside the pouch were folded pieces of paper covered in his spidery handwriting.

"Oh, it's beautiful," she said, blushing again. "But I wonder what happened to all of my letters?" she said, her voice quivering slightly. All that work, all that love, all that time she had put into writing them.

Rodrigo put his arm around her waist and they walked toward the airport exit. "Mail takes at least three weeks, and I was gone less than that. But, I've asked Adelmo to forward them to me when they arrive," he said. "Now, tell me what you've been doing without me here these weeks," he said, squeezing her close.

Some of the people passing by looked askance at them— Laura guessed it was because of Rodrigo's dark colored skin, but she didn't care. She was as happy as she had ever been.

As the spring semester advanced, the weather turned fiercely cold outside and treacherous black ice coated sidewalks, streets and paths, so it was not surprising that their dates led to them spending more time at Rodrigo's apartment. The bitter Chicago winds howled like wild dogs running hungrily through the forest, and the great lake froze over. Enormous leaden clouds heaped fluffy mounds of snow onto the city, and the two lovers cuddled on the couch and exchanged stories that had occurred when the air was warmer and friendlier.

"The first time I remember hearing about a country called the United States was in fifth grade," he said. "The

American embassy gifted all of the classrooms in our school with trash cans that said P-U-S-H on the lids. Naturally, we assumed that 'push' meant 'trash' in English."

"No!" Laura squealed with laughter.

"We did," he assured her, his eyes twinkling. "When someone had to throw something away, he would say 'I'm going to throw it in the push.' And there was this one boy, Guillermo Villanueva, who had really bad breath. So we called him 'push mouth.' Then I moved here to this lovely city," he said, waving his arm to take in the surroundings, "and one day I needed to go to a store. On the entrance door I saw the word 'PUSH.' I couldn't even go inside! By now I knew that it meant something else, of course, but in my heart, in my gut, it still had the original meaning, and I could not go inside and buy anything in a store that announced that it was trash on the front door."

Laura giggled and put her arms around her boyfriend. He was so good at telling her funny stories. Her stories were not as entertaining, she feared, but she shared her hunting adventures and other fun times, embellishing them as needed. She told him about the dogs she'd had on the farm. They were mostly working dogs, for protecting and herding the cattle and keeping the coyotes away, but one of them, Max, had puppies one year when Laura was about eight years old. Her parents gave away all but one, and that little guy, Pointer, grew up with them.

He was full of energy and he got into a lot of trouble. He had a penchant for chewing and if any tools with wooden handles got left out, he would chew them up. Her older brother, Henry, almost cried when he found that the handle of his good hammer, that had cost him $1.25, was reduced to pulp.

"We'll make a new handle for it and it'll be good as new," said her other brother, John. The new handle was nice but Henry said that it never fit as well on the iron head of the hammer as the original one had.

130

The dog also got into the bags of corn, chewing through the burlap and releasing the hard, white kernels. "Awfully big mice we've got around here," said her mother cheerily and sewed the hole in the bag. After that, they stored the bags up on a shelf with some bricks in front to keep the dog out.

And in the winter, one time they opened the back door to call Pointer for his dinner. A fresh blanket of snow had fallen and there were no dog tracks anywhere. As they shouted his name for several minutes, they began fearing that he had succumbed to the cold or that a coyote had gotten him. But then, right next to the barn door, the snow began to shift and Pointer rose up, his fur thick and white around him. He shook at least six inches of snow off, scattering it like seeds of a dandelion blowing off in the wind.

"I'm not sure I believe that," Rodrigo said teasingly.

"Scouts honor. Also, for some reason, Pointer loved lying down in my mother's petunias, and in no time he had flattened the whole flower bed."

"Did your mother get angry at him?"

"No, it was the strangest thing. She could stand having the dog commit all kinds of transgressions that she never tolerated in any of us."

"Aw," said Rodrigo playfully. "Poor little thing."

Laura threw a cushion at him.

Chapter 18

El Salvador, 1963

Sesi

I stayed at the doctor's house for five years. They were kind to me, *Don* Germán and *Doña* Flor Maria, his wife. They were quiet people who led a quiet life, with few changes day in and day out. They were an older couple and their one daughter lived far away in Santana and rarely came to visit.

I learned the routine and made myself useful around the house. It was just one other *muchacha*, whose name was Alma, and me working there. Alma did not live at the house because she was older and had a family, so she came and went each day.

Since she spent less time at the house than I did, I ended up having more chores to keep me busy, but the people were kind and I felt very fortunate, so I didn't mind. I washed clothes, ironed, dusted and swept every day, along with some light cooking duties. Like Miranda, Alma was primarily a cook, but she was wanting to take off more weekends, so the couple wanted a second cook. I wasn't that good in the beginning, but I got better under Alma's watchful eye. She would say things like, "Today we will learn how to boil eggs perfectly," or "Today we will make a perfect salad." Her method of teaching me little things like that really helped. When I got good at those things she moved onto harder things, like making tamales from scratch or stuffed bell peppers. I have a hard ear and clumsy hands because it took me a long time to learn well, but with her patient tutelage we finally made progress.

My favorite time of the day was the evenings, once the work was all done. That's when *Doña* Flor Maria let me read her books. She had a wonderful library which included all of the books from when her daughter had been little, and it was with these that I began. I read the sentences and then looked at the beautiful pictures, turning the pages reverently after I'd thoroughly exhausted the images with my eyes. A year later I moved on to novels, though it took me a long time to read them at first. I worked at it diligently though, as I loved stories.

At the end of the second year of my stay at her house we found that we quite enjoyed talking about what we read. She would make suggestions, pulling several books out at a time and sitting them on a side-table for me to look at. I would take each one, always singly, and read it in its entirety before returning it to take the next one. There were such wonderful stories and sometimes I wished that I had known them earlier so I could have shared them with Sara instead of filling her head with nonsensical stories like The Monkey Princess.

In this manner, cooking with Alma and reading with *Doña* Flor Maria, several years passed very quickly. They were very good years, but then in 1963 my life changed profoundly. I met a man and fell in love. It was a good kind of love like Mariángeles had with her prince, but unlike what happened in that story we did not get a chance to live happily ever after. I should not have expected it—that was just a child's story and I guess deep down I must have known that it would never happen that way to me. I even told myself that I was okay with that because I also knew that my face would never become all hairy like a monkey's if I happened to meet an evil river spirit and anger him by rebuffing him. Real life is like that—not nearly as spectacular although the bad things that happen can be really,

really bad.

At that time, things were becoming more violent than before in El Salvador. There had always been poverty, that was not new, but the poor used to always be able to find a way to survive. However, in the decade or so leading up to this time, something changed and that made everything worse. What happened was that the wealthy people began building fences around their land. This may not sound profound to you, but it is because of this single act, repeated on the land all over my country, that things were made much, much harder for the average person to survive.

Even when I was alone and destitute I could always find some fruit trees that would feed me. That's what everyone did. God made millions of mango trees and *marañon* trees and so on so that everyone could always have something to eat, no matter how poor they were. The fences changed everything.

The thing is, poor and uneducated people tolerate indignities and accept hardships much better than the rich people do, which is probably why there are so few rich people and so many poor people. I think that's what it is. But, you can push people so much, and then that's it. At a certain point, when a person can no longer hope to feed her family no matter how hard she works, when a man has no way of being useful no matter how hard he tries, when parents watch their children die of diarrhea before they are even one-year-old because the water is poisonous to them, and when those same people don't have to look far to see other people living a life of luxury and privilege, a life of wanton wastefulness and a life from which they (the wealthy people) can no longer see their fellow citizens for the humans that they are or notice or care for their suffering, well, people get good and mad. And when they do, they fight back using whatever weapons they have. If all they have are machetes, that's what they use. It's an ugly thing, but you can't really blame them.

134

And here's the other thing. When those people who are living in their luxurious houses and driving their expensive cars and giving their spoiled kids more money to spend buying firecrackers for the New Year's Eve celebrations than what they pay their *muchachas* for an entire month's worth of work, when these very same people see that the poor people are rising up, they get very frightened and in their angst, they strike hard. They strike mercilessly and brutally and fight like wild, rabid beasts to protect their way of life, decimating any and all who stand in their way.

And then both sides go at it even more madly and brutally and you end up with a civil war on your hands.

But, I was not thinking about this at the time. What I was thinking about was much more mundane and concrete and superbly exciting—I was thinking about boys. And not just boys in general, but one boy in particular. I was seventeen years old and wildly in love for the first time in my life.

I met Figo—that wasn't his real name, but it was the nickname that everyone called him—when I was at the market. He saw me first and started following me around, kind of like a lost puppy. Other than Enrique, no man had ever expressed overt interest in me. And honestly, I think Enrique should not count, since he was woman crazy all the time. So the fact that Figo was interested in me made it much easier to look past his unshaven chin and his unkempt hair that was a little too long. These things really bothered Alma, but I didn't mind them so much.

As my relationship with Figo blossomed with more and more mutual fondness, I found myself finishing my chores early and asking for permission to leave the house on longer and longer errands. I was very careful to always return before sunset, as a decent woman should, and I never left before all of my responsibilities were addressed. The doctor and his wife were kind to me. I think *Doña* Flor Maria guessed my amorous wanderings, or maybe it was Alma who told her about them, but she did not hinder me.

And so it was that Figo and I took longer walks into the parks, drinking in the heady perfume of the flowering Maquilishuat trees with their heavy pink blossoms and listening to the flocks of insane parakeets that chattered incessantly as they danced from branch to branch overhead. He told me funny jokes and I told him stories. When I told him the story of the Monkey Princess he said that it was our story, except that the roles were reversed, and that if I stayed with him, he would turn into a handsome man someday.

Figo had grown up poor, like me, but he was very smart and he was studying. He had finished high school and was in his second year at the university. He wanted to be an engineer, the kind that builds things. He would talk about building highways that stood on tall bridges and cut through mountains so that cities could be linked and travel time could be cut to a third of what it was today. He also talked about the fences and the ideas I just told you about. He belonged to a student group that discussed land reforms and dreamed of a future where more people could own the land instead of having it belong to only a few. He talked about unions and people having rights and elections not being rigged. I guess you could say he was very politically active, though at the time, I don't think I would have used those words.

I listened happily, more interested in having him tell me his excited dreams than in actually understanding them. Like I said, I was in silly love with him and all I wanted to do was spend lots of time together.

Figo loved it that I knew how to read. He said that's how he picked me out at the market that day—he saw me sit down to eat a *pupusa* and pull out a book to read while I waited. He said I was a dream-come-true, so clever and so pretty. I drank his compliments up like a thirsty river after the dry season.

136

When Figo said that he wanted me to consider going back to school too, I told him that I would love nothing more. So right then and there he began to make plans for our future. We decided that once he finished his degree and got a good job I would quit my job at the doctor's house and take classes to get a high school degree. After that, I could enroll at the university and get a degree there too. He even talked to me about things I could study and tried to help me find my interests. When all of my answers led to books, he said I should major in literature and write stories for a living. It seemed perfect. So you can see why I loved Figo so much.

It was Figo who first noticed that my tummy was stretching my dress—I had staunchly refused to acknowledge that there was anything different happening with my body. I guess it was part of my general delirium of being in love. You know how it is when you are running and you bump yourself and you don't even notice it and then two days later you see the bruise and can't even remember where or how you got it? It was kind of like that, but much more intense.

Deep down, I guess I knew that what we were doing was risky, but I was so happy and so busy, trying to work as fast as I could to get out of the house and be with him, that I ignored everything else. When we did the reckoning as to the last time I had bled, he tipped my head up and looked into my eyes.

"You will be a terrific mother," he said, "and I would be honored if you would let me be your husband."

Honestly, I felt like I really was in a fairy tale, it was so wonderful. I felt like I was the luckiest woman in the world.

We broke the news of my pregnancy, because you can't keep that a secret for too long once your tummy decides to rat on you, and *Doña* Flor Maria and *Don* Germán gave us their blessing. We planned to get married in a month's time. It would be a quick affair, and then we were going to live with Figo's cousin, Chema, who worked in construction.

But life isn't a fairy tale and happy times have a tendency to forget to stay happy. That was the lesson I thought I knew, but I had to learn it again, the hard way.

One morning, about a week before the wedding, I was working quietly in the back room of the house. I remember clearly, the way you do when a crisis strikes and you remember exactly what you were doing at the time you learn the news. I was folding the rags that were used for cleaning and dusting when I heard Alma call me. She was very pale and looked like she had seen a ghost. I could also see that she had been crying. Her eyes were bloodshot and her breath was hiccupy. I put my arm around her and asked her what was wrong. Then she looked at me and it was the saddest look any human being had ever given me. My heart immediately froze since I knew it meant that something really awful had occurred.

"What happened?" I whispered.

She began crying again and gave me a hug. Then she told me the worst story I ever hope to hear in my life.

"I went out for eggs this morning," she said. "I only had a few left and I thought the good doctor might want eggs for breakfast since Thursdays are his hospital days. I was running a little late so I took a shortcut to the *mercado*. And I saw..." Her voice broke off and she shook her head and began crying in earnest again.

"What did you see?" I prompted in my innocence, but I think even my baby knew that the problem was ours as she began kicking fiercely. Or maybe it was that I was clenching my stomach in anticipation of what Alma would say. I knew that it had to be some awful news for Alma to be carrying on that way.

"In the gutter..." Alma's voice was nearly a whisper.

I was already feeling that I probably did not want to hear

138

what it was that she had seen and I was trying to think of a good way to take back my words. The reports about the killings perpetrated by the *Escuadrones de la Muerte*, the government-backed Death Squads, had been so gruesome lately. Everyone was talking about them, though I had not actually seen anything personally. Then again, I rarely left the house early in the morning and that's when these crimes were discovered.

Alma's shoulders heaved for a few minutes as I patted her back and made comforting sounds.

"You don't have to tell me," I said gently. By this time, I was completely convinced that I did not want to hear her story.

She lifted her apron and dabbed at her face. "What I saw in the gutter was a young man's head. Figo..."

I felt like I was going to be sick. I quickly covered her mouth with my hands as my stomach convulsed. Then I ran to the sink and was sick, multiple times. And in between the tears that poured out of my eyes like the afternoon rains, I wretched and puked some more. It was the worst I had ever felt in my entire life. I didn't even know that someone could feel so utterly devastated, so completely heartbroken. If someone had taken a machete to me and cut me up, right there, like a coconut, I don't think it would have hurt more.

I wretched and cried for a long time. *Doña* Flor Maria came into the kitchen and found us crying and Alma told her what happened and then she cried too. The doctor did not get his breakfast that morning.

After a long time of crying, I don't know how long, I lay my head on the table and didn't move. My whole body ached. My chest felt like it wanted to break apart, my stomach was one large bruise, and my head was splitting. Alma led me to my cot and fed me broth but I kept throwing up as soon as I would get more than a few spoonsful in my stomach.

139

That evening the doctor came to me and gave me some medicine that made me go to sleep. When I woke up in the middle of the next day, I still hurt everywhere, but I was able to hold food down. However, I was in no mood to eat. I wanted so badly to be with Figo again that I was thinking that if I died, that would be a good thing. But between Alma, *Doña* Flor Maria and the Doctor, they didn't let me die.

They took turns prodding, nagging and cajoling me, for days on end, to keep eating. But I didn't feel like it. All my zest for life was gone. Then they said that Figo was watching from heaven and he would be pretty upset with me if I didn't take care of his baby. I thought about that and it made sense. So I finally started eating, slowly, and returning to the realm of the survivors.

It was more than two weeks later when I finally got the rest of the details from Alma. She didn't want to tell me because she was afraid that I would fall back into depression, but when I reassured her that I would live and I really wanted to know, she told me things like how his face was bloody and scarred, with cigarette burns all over. Even on his eyes. How can people be so cruel? I will never, ever understand.

When Alma first came upon his severed head, all she saw was the hair and she thought, for just a second, that it was a large rat or a rabbit. But then she looked again and she saw the rest of his face and realized that she knew him.

For months I hoped and prayed, and at times truly expected, that it was not Figo that she had seen. As my tummy continued to stubbornly grow, I would look for him everywhere I went, hoping against hope to get a glimpse of him. I even went to his cousin Chema's house, but I turned around when I saw his face and the hollowness of his eyes that confirmed the story Alma had told me.

I was so sad for so long that I thought my little baby, his

little baby, would surely die inside of me. And often, especially at night, I would wonder how I could go on nurturing a life when the only one I had ever cared for had been so brutally taken away from me.

I would very much like to tell you that this was the only time I brushed close to the horrible, blood-curdling events that shook my country for the next decade. But I cannot honestly do that. The gruesomeness and horror are beyond my ability to portray and probably beyond your ability to comprehend, if for no other reason than the fact that our minds close down when we are faced with such inhuman brutality.

Chapter 19

Illinois, 1963

Laura

It was April and Laura's period was late. She always kept an eye on the calendar so as not to be caught by surprise, but she had been carrying pads around in her purse for over two weeks now and she was trying not to think of what that could mean. Then one morning she woke up and felt sick to her stomach. She immediately guessed the reason and began to sweat with fear.

What would happen to her now? She hadn't even told her parents that she was dating anyone. What if Rodrigo changed his mind about her? She could end up alone. Or she might have to give her baby up for adoption and never see it again. And how would she finish college if she was pregnant?

These questions pecked at her all morning long, like hens protecting their eggs. By the time she went to work at the bakery that afternoon, the questions had multiplied and when she felt sick again, she wasn't sure if it was because of what was in her uterus or what was in her head. She excused herself from kneading the bread and went to the toilet. When she emerged, Laura senior, who had eyes sharper than a hawk's, called her over.

"Let me have a look at you," she said kindly.

Laura glanced furtively around the kitchen and was relieved that no one else was around.

Laura senior held the back of her hand up to Laura's forehead for a few seconds. "No fever. And you look pale. Dark circles under your eyes. You're breathing through your nose— that's good. Throat hurt?"

Laura shook her head.

"Hm," she said, putting her hands on her broad hips and frowning as she thought. "How are things going with that boy you were seeing, that foreigner?"

Laura had not spoken to her boss about her continued romance with Rodrigo since she knew that her boss did not approve of their courtship, but at the mention of him, she blushed.

"Oh! Oh, no! Laura! Don't tell me you're gonna have a baby!"

Laura blushed more deeply and suddenly tears sprung to her eyes. Rodrigo was finishing his senior project for his civil engineering degree and they had not spent much time together in the last ten days, so he did not know that her period was late.

"Oh! Oh, dear! Oh, my goodness!" Laura senior seemed to be at a loss for words. "Well, nothing you can do about it now. Dear me. Have you told your folks back home?"

Laura shook her head.

"Oh, golly. Well, you're gonna have to tell them. Best if you could arrange the wedding as soon as possible. That is if he'll marry you. I hope he isn't a cad. Do you think he'll marry you?"

Tears began leaking from Laura's eyes as she shrugged her reply.

"You haven't told him you've got a bun in the oven?"

143

Laura shook her head.

"Oh, dearie me. Well, you need to tell him as soon as possible. And let's hope he's a good one, but if not, we'll come up with another plan. In the meantime, sweetie, I hate to have to tell you, but as soon as you start showing, I won't be able to let you serve the customers up front, or even have anyone see you working here in the back unless you get a wedding ring on that finger of yours. You know how it is," she said, making a face.

Laura nodded.

"Oh, you poor dear," Laura senior said, giving Laura a quick hug. "There now. Go wash yourself up and we'll talk more about it afterwards. We have five pies waiting to go in the oven and now's not the time. Oh, dear! I hope he's a gentleman, Laura. I don't even want to think about what will happen if he doesn't want you!"

After work that night, Laura went to Rodrigo's apartment. He was not there, but she had a key and let herself in. She fell asleep on the bed before he got home, and woke up in his arms.

"To what do I owe this surprise visit?" he said, nuzzling her ear as the sun's rays snuck through the window blinds.

"Rodrigo," she said, remembering her mission. She sat up and leaned on one arm. "I have something important to tell you. I'm going to have a baby."

Rodrigo's shock lasted only a second and was immediately replaced by his warm smile. "A baby! Our baby. Well, it's sooner than I had hoped, but it's still wonderful news. A little Rodrigo junior. How far along are you?"

Laura told him the date of her last period and he counted on his fingers. She was a little surprised at how well he was handling the situation, but it also helped to calm her nerves and confirm in her heart that she had chosen a good man.

Rodrigo got out of bed and grabbed a calendar from off the desk. "Let's see," he said, sitting down next to her again. "You will be due at the start of next year. So, that means you probably won't show before the summer. I've got several more weeks of classes left in the school year. How about if we get married in May, right after I graduate?"

Her wedding proposal was rather more business-like than Laura had dreamed it would be, but circumstances dictated it. She nodded and he hugged her again.

"I love you, future Mrs. Arechavaleta," he said tenderly. "May I measure your finger?"

She nodded and then immediately covered her mouth and ran to the bathroom to throw up.

Breaking the news about Rodrigo to her parents was a challenging affair that Laura did not anticipate would go well. Having neglected to tell them that she was even dating Rodrigo, she would have a lot of explaining to do.

With Sally visiting Laura in Chicago for the weekend, the three of them went to a local diner to plan Laura's next steps. They sat in the booth and discussed the matter over hamburgers and shakes.

"I think I'll just call them on the telephone," Laura announced, not making eye contact with her sister or her fiancé.

Both Sally and Rodrigo thought that was a bad idea.

"You need to tell them in person," Rodrigo said in a soothing tone.

"But I wouldn't mention the pregnancy," Sally added.

"Let them get over the first shock before giving them a second one," agreed Rodrigo.

145

"I'll go home the same weekend and be with you," Sally said. "For moral support."

Laura turned in her seat and embraced her sister. "I owe you," she said gratefully into her sister's hair.

"Nonsense," said Sally. "Sisters stick together."

"Well, I knew something was up when the two of you announced you'd be coming home the same weekend when there was no cause for it," said Laura's mother. "But a foreigner, Laura Maria, what got into you?"

It was Saturday morning and Laura and Sally had arrived back at the farm an hour ago. It had been a very dry spring and even the weeds, which were normally a fresh green color, hung limp with thirst.

Laura kept her eyes downcast. There was such a gulf between her and her mother that she could not even begin to bridge it.

"He's a really nice guy, Mom. I've met him," said Sally.

"You met him and you never thought to tell me about it?" said her mother.

Sally crossed her arms and looked away, past her father and outside where Pointer, now old and arthritic, was sunning himself on the dusty ground.

"Catholic?" her mother barked.

"Yes, ma'am."

"Well, at least that. I expect you'd better go talk to Father Dick and ask him to reserve a time in the church for a May wedding," she said.

Laura nodded.

"And don't expect your Pop and me to pay for nothing.

146

Times are tight enough as it is without having to spend money we hadn't planned."

Laura shook her head. Under the table, Sally reached for Laura's hand and squeezed it.

Laura's father said nothing. He sat at the table and poked at his pipe and generally ignored all the females in the room.

On Sunday, Laura and Sally stayed after mass to speak with the priest, and then that afternoon, the sisters embraced and said their goodbyes.

Chapter 20

Illinois, 1963

Laura

On a fine, bright morning in May, Rodrigo and Laura were married. It was a small ceremony, consisting only of her immediate family and a few of their friends from college. The mass was predicated by a sour-faced priest. Father Dick was a cousin to Laura's mother and seemed to have inherited the same dour outlook on life.

Rodrigo was immaculate, in a white suit with a white shirt and tie and shiny white shoes. Laura wore a dress she borrowed from her cousin Sylvia, Jimmy's older sister, who had gotten married the year before. Sally wore a cherry pink dress and beamed as if it was the happiest day of her life.

Laura senior had helped Laura to hem the dress the week before. She also attended the wedding, providing a ray of sunshine despite her previous misgivings about Rodrigo. "I guess if you love him and he loves you, that's all that matters," she had said. She also surprised the couple with a lovely three-tiered wedding cake laden with small yellow roses made of sugar.

"You're the best friend I could have asked for," said

148

Laura to her boss. "Thank you for everything!"

Also at the ceremony was Rodrigo's closest friend from El Salvador, Adelmo. Laura had heard so much about Adelmo that she felt as if she already knew him, and she was thrilled to finally meet him in person. Adelmo was shorter than Rodrigo, with high cheekbones and darker brown eyes. His hair was straight and his lips, which broke into smiles often, were very thin.

Sally was Laura's maid of honor, and Adelmo was Rodrigo's best man. At some point before the wedding began, Laura's mother made a snarky comment about the fact that Rodrigo's parents had not come to the wedding. She said it loud enough that most of the people heard her.

Laura blushed, feeling bad for Rodrigo since his father was deceased. She knew that his mother had wanted to attend, but the journey would have been very long as she did not live in the capital city. In the end, she had gifted the couple with the money she would have spent on traveling to the wedding, and Rodrigo was planning to save the money for when the baby came.

"With all due respect, ma'am," said Laura senior in her no-nonsense tone, "I can't help but wonder if you and your husband would have made the trip if Laura had gotten married in Chicago, let alone Central America?"

Laura felt both frightened and elated at her friend's comment and worried that her mother would make a scene before the wedding began, but instead she put her nose up in the air and turned away.

When Laura looked at her boss, Laura senior winked at her and Laura felt a gush of relief flowing through her.

For their honeymoon, Rodrigo took Laura on a cross-country drive to Mount Rushmore. They drove slowly, stopping at small roadside hotels along the way. From Chicago, they headed north to Minneapolis and stayed there for a few days. Then they headed southwest, driving through Minnesota, with its endless number of lakes and great forests. It was still chilly, but spring was in the air and the leaves were a fresh shade of green. From there they drove to South Dakota.

Laura was fascinated with the giant stone faces that were far larger than she had imagined. As an engineer, Rodrigo was very interested to find out how it had been done. He read up on the construction of the monument and then regaled Laura with stories about how they had constructed the heads.

"First they made the head of George Washington. His head took seven years because the country was going through an economic depression. Then they started on Jefferson's head, but it didn't look good because the rock was not the right kind, so they dynamited it away."

"No, that can't be right," said Laura.

"Yes, they destroyed it and then made the new head on Washington's left side."

Laura wasn't sure if he was kidding, but she later found out that her new husband had been telling her the truth.

"How long did it take to make Jefferson?"

"Just two years. Then they made Lincoln's head, but they had a lot of trouble with his beard. Still, they finished it the following year, in 1937, and then two years later they made the last one, Theodore Roosevelt."

On the way back to Chicago, the newlyweds first headed south, stopping in Sioux City and then they drove to Des Moines, before turning back northward.

150

Laura began to show right after the wedding, and they passed through endless miles of cornfields and farms, her morning sickness persisted. Her doctor had approved the road trip on the condition that she "take it easy," and "come back and see me as soon as you get back."

They had postponed telling her parents about the pregnancy until after the honeymoon. That was a good thing because it turned out that there was a surprising reason the doctor was so eager to see her as soon as she got back.

"You are having twins," he announced.

Rodrigo was excited and proud to learn that he had fathered two children at once, but Laura was overwhelmed.

"Twins," she said as they drove home from the doctor's office. "I'll never finish college now."

"I've been thinking about that," Rodrigo said, keeping one hand on the steering wheel and taking her hand with his other one. "You are so close to finishing now, only two semesters. I have an idea."

And so it was that Laura took summer classes to get ahead, and then graduated in December. Her parents did not come to her graduation, which was a relief to Laura. In attendance were her friends, Sally and Laura senior, who showed up with a long, thin cake that looked like a diploma, tied in icing shaped like string.

Chapter 21

El Salvador, 1964

Sesi

When my belly was quite ripe, and *Doña* Flor Maria felt it and saw that the contractions were strong and regular, she told me that the baby would be here at any moment. Then *Don* Germán arranged for a midwife to come to the house and help with the delivery. That was so very kind of them to care for me like that! My little girl came out healthy and happy and I thanked the Blessed Virgin Mary for that gift.

During my pregnancy, I spent many nights awake, afraid that I might not be able to love my baby when she came out. I know that sounds strange, but I was so heartbroken about losing Figo that I felt like I could never love anyone else. I felt like a cricket who would never be able to sing its happy song into the night again.

To my great relief, when I saw my little baby, I instantly fell in love with her. She had big, dark eyes and mounds of coffee-colored brown hair whose wispy edges curled defiantly in all directions. Her deeply arched eyebrows were also just like her daddy's.

My little daughter was a miracle. I called her "Rocio"

(which means "dew") because that was Figo's mother's name and he talked highly of her. She passed away five years ago, so I never got to meet her. But I wish I could have. I would have thanked her for raising such a good, kind man.

Rocio nursed every two hours around the clock and after a few days I was in a walking dream, dizzy with lack of sleep. It seemed the only thing she did was take fluids in and immediately put them back out. I marveled that she even had time to digest anything. But mostly I fought to steal even a few minutes to sleep as I was very weak. I had never been heavy and my baby seemed to be draining my very soul from me.

When things were looking really bad, and little Rocio was crying all the time because she was still hungry and I was in tears because my cracked, sore nipples gave more blood than milk, Alma found a friend who had extra milk. She was rather larger of build and on her third child, and soon I was able to sleep for five or six hours in a row.

I got back to work as soon as I was able to, but it became clear that having my tiny baby at work did not let me do what I needed to do. I put her in a sling on my back and tried to keep up with the work, but no matter how hard I tried, it was not enough. My daughter would cry and I would be torn between stopping to take care of her, or finishing the task at hand. If the choice was between my comfort and the work, the work always won, but it was hard to choose work over Rocio as she had loud vocal chords. Also, I felt really guilty if I had to ask her to wait to eat or have her bottom dried.

So I was not surprised when *Doña* Flor Maria had a talk with me. I had just weaned Rocio, and she was six months old.

"I'll understand if you want to leave this house and go live with your mother and daughter," she said kindly.

But I knew that my mother could not afford to take us both in. She could handle the baby for a few years, she had made

153

that clear, but not me. And there was not enough work for me in the village where I had grown up.

I stayed with my mother for a few days, to get the baby used to her and the other way around. My mother and I didn't speak much—it was the way we were—but one afternoon she reminded me again that I would make more money in the capital. As she spoke she glanced towards Linda's mother's house, which now sported a new veranda and had recently been repainted.

"They say she'll be putting in indoor plumbing and a tiled bathroom," my mother said wistfully.

I put my head down and thanked her for keeping my baby. The next day I went back to Santa Tecla.

Chapter 22

Illinois, 1964

Laura

In January, 1964, Lyndon Johnson, who took over as President of the United States after Kennedy's assassination in November, gave his first State of the Union Address. Plans to build the New York City World Trade Center were announced, and The Beatles were just about to hit the #1 spot on the U.S. singles chart for the first time. Meanwhile, in the small country from which Rodrigo came, Colonel Julio A. Rivera Carballo, an oligarch, had recently been elected president under the sham of a democracy.

Over the phone, Laura's mother offered to come and help the first week when the twins arrived, but it was a half-hearted offer, and Laura heard the relief in her mother's voice when she told her mother that she probably wouldn't need the help.

Laura had been on strict bed-rest since graduating the second week in December. "Twins often want to come early," the doctor had warned, "and we want them to stay and grow as much as possible, so you have to be very careful."

"I feel like an elephant," she complained.

Rodrigo passed his finger tenderly over her belly button,

which had turned inside out and protruded at the top of her belly. "You are a beautiful volcano incubating our two precious children," he said.

"You're comparing me to a mountain. That doesn't make me feel better," said Laura.

Finally, on a snowy day in the third week of January, Laura woke up to find the bed all wet and her belly becoming stiff and squeezing in regular intervals. Her children, whose movement had become much less over the last few days, were now practically not moving at all.

"Wake up, Rodrigo, it's time."

Rodrigo was not a morning person and she had to shove him again after a few moments.

"Wake up! We gotta go!" she said.

He sat up and turned pale. "Are you sure?"

"Yes! Help me get up or we'll have the babies right here."

Rodrigo threw on some clothes, grabbed her overnight bag and escorted her out the door. He was as white as a sheet as he drove to the hospital, ignoring most of the lights as well as the speed limit. But Laura was in too much pain to tell him to slow down. They pulled up in front of the hospital and Rodrigo ran inside to get help. The orderlies were not in too much of a hurry when they saw him, but when they made it out to the car and found a blonde woman with a huge belly, they sprang into action.

The birth took only two hours as she was very dilated and the babies were on the small side, weighing just over five pounds each. The little girl, Isabella, was slightly larger than the little boy, Rodrigo Junior. When the nurse told Rodrigo that all

156

was well and his new family was ready to meet him, Rodrigo's eyes rolled to the back of his head and he swayed. Luckily the nurse had seen this reaction before and she was quick on her feet. Another orderly who just happened to be walking by also saw what was happening and between the two of them, they managed to keep Rodrigo from injuring himself badly as he fell to the floor.

"What happened to you?" Laura asked when she saw the bandage on his forehead.

"I...I was so worried...and when they said everything was all right, and the babies, I...I guess I—"

"Good grief," said Laura, smiling fondly at her husband. He really was such a great guy and she was so happy.

For the first few months after the twins were born, Sally came and stayed most weekends. On the other days, Laura's friends made a point to stop by, and Laura senior came every week, bringing several meat pies and other pre-made food that could be frozen so that the new parents would not have to cook.

In retrospect, Laura did not know what she would have done without her sister and her friends and kind employer. The twins took a lot of energy and time. It was a good thing that Laura was young and used to working hard.

The doctor strongly advised that she wean them onto baby formula rather quickly, which was fine by her. Then she got busy tending to all their physical needs. She bought a double stroller in the Salvation Army store and took the children out as soon as the weather would allow. Spring came and soon it was summer and both children were blossoming into chubby, beautiful babies.

Chapter 23

El Salvador, 1965-1969
Sesi

At *Doña* Flor Maria's house, I worked extra hard. She and *Don* Germán were very kind and every other week they gave me a day and a half off so that I could travel home by bus and be with my baby. I saved all my money for the bus rides and for my mother

The two-hour bus ride was insufferably long on my way to see my little Rocio, and alarmingly quick as it swept me back to work each Sunday night. Sometimes the brightly painted bus would break down and we would have to wait for hours for another bus to come. If this happened on my way to see Rocio I would curse my luck, but if it happened on the way back to the doctor's house I would spend the time reliving each milestone of my daughter's growth that I had seen.

And so the years stumbled by on heavy feet. The trouble was that I became spoiled and I wanted more. As my daughter grew to be a toddler, and then began talking and discovering her world, my heart broke more and more each time I had to leave her. She changed so much in two weeks between our visits that each time I saw her, I had to get to know her all over again. And she had to get to know me too. She would be a little shy for the first hour and I had to treat her like a kitty cat, pretending that I was not that interested in her while she watched me closely. After that she would warm up to me and let me hold her. Fortunately, as my little Rocio grew older, she learned to remember me and the time it took for us to get reacquainted decreased.

But I missed a lot of her childhood in those years. I missed her teeth popping their little white heads out of her gums. I missed her very first wet kisses, her open mouth pressed briefly on my mother's cheek. I missed the first time she said "Ma." I missed her first tentative steps and nursing her when she had colds. I missed her transition out of diapers and her delight the first time she tasted a piece of soft, yellow mango.

Figo missed all of these milestones too. And what's more, he was not there to see the little white tooth clearly poking through her gums or feel her second wet kiss or hear her chant "Ma-Ma-Ma" with growing confidence or step across the room, waffling to keep erect, or getting more mango on her face than in her mouth. I did have those opportunities.

But still, when my little Rocio turned four years old I cried violently the entire bus journey back to work. Instead of it getting easier over time to leave my little girl, I found that I really could not stand to be apart from her any longer.

At least once a year I had asked *Doña* Flor Maria if there was any way I could bring Rocio to live with us at the house, but each time she gently apologized. That's why, although I was happily employed, paid and treated well, I finally took my mother's advice and went back to my original plan of moving to San Salvador.

The capital city was close by now, so I began looking for another place to work without having to quit my current job, so I could keep making money. Of course, that also meant that it took a lot longer to find a place. And, I had to do it carefully, not wanting to upset *Doña* Flor Maria and engender her wrath and a premature dismissal. I saved each cent to take back to my mother so she could buy things for Rocio—and there were always more things that were needed than what my meager wages provided.

When Rocio turned five years old, I finally got lucky and found a different job. I won't go into the serendipity of circumstances that cannot be anything other than the Virgin Mary's kind hand in my life, possibly because She had mercy on Rocio, growing up without a father and far from her mother who yearned for her constantly. Or maybe it was Figo himself, up in heaven, who went to argue with the Virgin and convince Her to do something. Once he got an idea in his head, he chattered more than the *pericos* until you finally gave in. Either way, since I don't believe in magic I'm convinced that there was intervention on my behalf. There can be no other explanation and I am extremely grateful for Her hand in my fate.

Chapter 24

Illinois, 1965

Laura

Once the immediate crisis of having two babies to feed, soothe and change became a routine, Laura had some time to reflect on her life. She loved her new family and her husband. Rodrigo worked long hours, and that meant that he didn't spend as much time with her and the children, but he was a new hire and he had to prove himself, so she allowed him the space that he needed.

But being dark-skinned man in white America was not an easy task. It had been nearly one hundred years since slavery ended, but prejudice was still rampant. Rodrigo was routinely judged on his appearances and it was very frustrating. At work, his boss dismissed his proposals without giving them a chance, then praised similar plans presented by lighter skinned employees.

He even went so far as to test his hypothesis: he drew up plans for the section of freeway, just south of the Great Lake, that was being designed by his firm. He took the plans to his boss and he was waved away. Then he gave his plans to his good friend Greg, who worked in the office next to Rodrigo. Greg erased Rodrigo's name and put the plan in his dossier and presented it to the same boss. This time the plan was received warmly, and the boss praised the insights of the plan. Both Greg and Rodrigo were surprised and dismayed that Rodrigo's test had worked, but neither dared to call attention to the experiment lest they both lose their jobs.

After that, Greg made a point of "teaming up" with Rodrigo, under the auspices of "helping him find his way" and the boss agreed that their work was "much better now that Greg was showing Rod the ropes."

But even that farce did not completely resolve the prejudice that Rodrigo faced. One day, after giving a presentation about his work to a client, the client remarked on how clever Rodrigo was.

"He was genuinely surprised that I could have a good idea, and be able to answer all of his questions with clear and creative solutions," Rodrigo told Laura. He was clearly frustrated that the client had not expected to find a thinking engineer under the dark skin.

"What'd you say?" Laura asked, rubbing his tired shoulders.

"I said, 'just because I speak with an accent, doesn't mean that I think with one.' "

Laura laughed. She loved how clever Rodrigo was.

"Things will get better, sweetheart. You're doing great work and they're going to see it," she said.

But Rodrigo just sighed and shook his head. "I miss my country," he said, his accent making the word sound like cone tree.

Chapter 25

Illinois, 1967

Laura

"I think we should move to El Salvador," Rodrigo said.

It was a Saturday afternoon in April and there were twenty inches of snow on the ground. Inside the apartment it was chilly enough that even with sweaters, everyone had red noses. The twins were now toddlers and they had been going all day. They were cranky and both needed fresh diapers but neither wanted to be caught for the diaper change. Laura looked at her husband, and then looked away. She was tired and hungry herself.

"We should move there, Laura. The weather is much nicer than here. And I could work at the university. I would make more money. We could have a bigger house. You would have help with the children. It would be a better life."

Laura listened and empathized, but she was surprised to find that she wasn't ready to leave Illinois after all. Somehow, having the babies had changed her mind about moving to a foreign country. The thought of leaving Sally and Laura senior and going where she would not know anyone was frightening. And then there was the matter of the language. She didn't know

163

any Spanish at all.

Plus, there was her career as a teacher, a dream she still nurtured. If she went to El Salvador, she did not know the language to teach at a school there. So, what would she do all day?

And what if they stayed there for years? Her children would miss being kids in America. No Halloween. No Easter egg hunts. No snow men or sled rides. Santa Claus in swimming trunks. Even though her own childhood had not been idyllic, she felt protective of theirs and wanted it to be the best she could possibly give them.

But, on the other hand, Rodrigo did have a point. He faced unkindness because of his skin color in more places than his work. On several occasions, she walked into a restaurant to order a table while Rodrigo was parking the car.

"Yes, ma'am, just a moment while we prepare it," the maître d' would say respectfully. But once Rodrigo joined her, the reservation would suddenly vanish.

"I'm awfully sorry, ma'am, but we no longer have a table available," she would be told by a waitress scowling at Rodrigo.

And, she reasoned, it had to be tough always speaking with an accent, always looking different, missing your friends? And, when she was honest with herself, she forced herself to remember how much she had longed to leave and go far away. She had been open to the idea of moving from the time she met Rodrigo.

Laura looked back at her husband and saw his pleading eyes. It made her feel wretched for holding back. She knew that he deserved better than what he was getting here.

"Can't we give it a few more years? Just till the twins turn four? Then we can talk about moving to El Salvador," she

164

said.

Rodrigo got up and left the room.

As Laura sat on the carpet, watching her twins fighting over a plastic ball, she rubbed her her arms, feeling as if she was pecked at by the chickens again. She really did not know what the right decision was. Maybe it wouldn't be so bad to move? But not now. The twins had just turned three. Isabella was out of diapers, but Junior still was not. Maybe next year?

It made her tired just to think about it. It was so unfair that a good man like Rodrigo could not get a fair shot here because of his skin color. She looked at her babies again. They were growing so fast. It seemed like just yesterday that they had taken their first wobbly steps and now they ran all over the apartment, reaching up to everything and pulling things down, putting things in their mouth. She smiled. Motherhood was exhausting, but there was also something very special about it— an unexpected delight. And speaking of motherhood, it was time to get busy again.

"All right, Junior, let's get you into a fresh diaper," she said, hauling herself up from the floor.

"Nooo," he squealed and ran toward the kitchen, his chubby bare feet pumping as fast as they could with the wet, heavy diaper flopping between his legs.

After dinner, Rodrigo helped her give the kids a bath and put them to bed. Then Laura and Rodrigo went to sit on the couch.

"Look, I'm really, sorry," she said. "I know you deserve better. Can we please just give the U.S. another year? If things aren't better by this time next year, we'll move to El Salvador. Is that all right?"

"Yes," he said.

The sadness etched in the creases of his eyes threatened

165

to break her heart.

Chapter 26

El Salvador, 1969

Sesi

For years, I had quietly and carefully put out the word that I was looking to move. One day a friend of a friend of an acquaintance heard that there was a family in the Cuscatlán area looking for a cook. Cuscatlán is one of the neighborhoods that belongs to the capital city of San Salvador. It was not very far from where I was, but I knew that taking that job would mean that I'd finally made it to the big city, my dream for so long, and that was appealing. It was kind of like a line in the sand, saying you worked in Cuscatlán instead of Santa Tecla, but it was an important line to me.

When I heard the name of the neighborhood—no one knew exactly which house it was—I took myself on a walk there. And that's where I saw the sign in the window. *"Se busca cocinera."* Now, I don't love to cook like Miranda did, but, thanks to Alma's tutelage, I do know my way around the kitchen so I did not hesitate when I saw that sign.

The note itself was unobtrusive, written in blue ink on a half sheet of paper and posted in the corner of the garage. Someone who didn't know how to read might have mistook it for a notice as to where to deliver the fresh tortillas that most people had taken to their front door, as some preferred to receive through a small door next to the garage.

I went straight up to the house and knocked purposefully. In just a few moments *Doña* Laura answered. For a moment I was dumbstruck. I had never seen such a chele—that is, such a white-skinned person—in all my life. Her skin was practically translucent. She was the color of unbaked bread and her eyes were the deep blue of the sky that had hung over the maquilishuat trees when I walked by them in the park, holding hands with Figo.

She greeted me, saying the words in a really funny way that reminded me of when Rocio was first learning to speak, and then she made some other unintelligible vocal sounds. I greeted her formally in return and enquired politely about the job, quickly listing my skills. When I finished she looked at me pleasantly but clearly puzzled and it hit me suddenly that, just as I could not understand her, she also could not understand me. Perhaps it was owing to her chele complexion, I thought, that she did not understand God's language.

I knew that other languages existed—my mother had told me of the Pilpil Indians and how they had spoken a different language many years ago, and I knew that deep in the forest there were still natives who did not speak Spanish. Figo had also told me of people who spoke other languages and were involved in the politics of our country, but I had never hoped to meet a person like this. I was so desperate for the job, though, that I had to figure something out. I remembered how once, a long time ago when I used to care for little Sara, she had been ill and unable to speak. I had decided to join in her silent state to make things more fun and we used miming motions to communicate. We were able to understand each other pretty well that way, so I figured it was worth it to try this with the chele. I pointed to the sign on the garage and then made motions that a cook would make, stirring a pot, peeling a jicama, and then pointed to myself. She smiled and nodded and I knew in that instant that we could be friends.

The one other thing I did was to make the motion of holding a baby, then point to myself. It was the one inviolable condition for me taking up employment elsewhere and the question needed to be asked up front. At that moment one of her two children, who was just a bit younger than Rocio, came up and wrapped her arms protectively around her mother's knees. The little girl was not chele like herself but had more normal colored skin, although her face clearly looked just like her mother's otherwise.

Doña Laura spoke in her unintelligible language, pointing to her daughter and to herself and then to me. I can't tell you how, but I understood that she had understood my question. I nodded solemnly, completely prepared to turn around and continue looking for somewhere else to work if her answer was 'no.'

She stood there for a moment, her eyes looking out at the roofs of the other houses. She was clearly thinking about my request and even though it wasn't particularly hot, I felt little trickles of sweat running down the sides of my face. Finally, she made the mime of putting her hand, palm down, on top of her child's head and then motioned at me. It took me a couple of seconds to figure out what she was trying to say because at first I thought she had misunderstood me and was asking how tall my pig was.

I don't have a pig or a dog or a horse. And everyone knows you only measure the height of animals with your palm down. But, then suddenly I realized that she was asking how big my child was. I showed her, keeping the palm of my hand flat, vertical and outward facing so as not to anger the spirits of growth who watched over Rocio and might stymie her potential height if they saw my palm facing downward to mark her height.

Then *Doña* Laura nodded her head, saying "*Sí,*" and we

both broke into huge smiles. I was ecstatic to finally be able to work in a place where I could have my little Rocio with me. I was also slightly overwhelmed to think that I had finally, finally landed a job in the capital city.

Then the chele did something that completely threw me off guard because none of my employers, even *Doña* Flor Maria with whom I was closer than any other previous employer, had ever done: she reached out and gave me a small, quick hug.

I was surprised and a tiny bit frightened and terrifically happy all at the same time. To be shown so much kindness from someone who wasn't even from El Salvador—for that much I had deduced by now—was something that I would never have expected. I would love to tell you how we arranged the time and date for me starting and moving to her place, but I'm sorry to say that those details have been lost forever. I was so giddy with delight and it was so new to me to be communicating with just gestures that I really have no idea.

I dreaded telling the doctor and *Doña* Flor Maria about my new working arrangements, but I should not have. They were very kind to me. I think *Doña* Flor Maria realized how sad I had been all that time not to have Rocio with me and she did not wish me ill. When I left the next day she pressed a bag of books on me and even gave me a few extra *colones*. To this day I go back and visit her when I get a chance and take her some pastries, if I can. There should be more people in the world like her.

As for how *Doña* Laura, who did not speak Spanish, came to live in San Salvador, I later learned that *Don* Rodrigo Manuel had lived for a time in the land of "gringos," way up north, and had gotten married there to one of the natives. From what *Doña* Laura explained, when she eventually learned enough Spanish for us to have more in-depth conversations, lots of people in her country up north looked like her, with pale skin and hair and fair eyes.

It wasn't that there was something physically wrong with her, which is what I had originally believed when she opened the door that day when I was nervously applying for the job, but rather that everyone up there was like that. She told me, and I will confess to you that I find this hard to believe, that *Don* Rodrigo Manuel, who I can tell you is the most ordinary looking man you could hope to meet on any street in El Salvador, had stood out in her land for being so dark. And the truth is that he's not that dark at all! He's just regular so it feels like sacrilege to even say that, but I trust *Doña* Laura now, and if she says that it was so, then she must be right.

Anyway, at some point *Don* Rodrigo Manuel decided that it was time to come back to El Salvador, which is understandable, and so he brought his wife and two kids with him. And I'm so glad he did and that I heard about this opening and that *Doña* Laura understood me and accepted me and my daughter because all of this changed my life profoundly.

171

Chapter 27

El Salvador, 1968

Laura

In the spring of 1968 Rodrigo declared again that he wanted to move to El Salvador and this time she felt that she could not deny him. She still didn't know any Spanish, the twins were ready to start kindergarten and she had never left Illinois, but she screwed her eyes tightly shut and jumped into her new role as a house wife in an exotic land.

It was what she had always dreamed of, wasn't it? Hadn't she, throughout all of her life, prayed for hours on end to be able to move far, far away from Illinois? Well here was her dream, coming true and slapping her hard in the face.

The day Laura arrived with her two children and her husband in El Salvador and heard everyone, everywhere talking in Spanish and saw that all of the signs on the street were in Spanish, she wondered what she had gotten herself into. There was nothing from her former life that could have prepared her for the new reality of life in El Salvador. She had listened to her husband's stories about growing up and she had tried to imagine what it would be like, but it was like trying to imagine a fairy tale world or living on another planet.

He told her of the time when he was about four years old and he asked his mother if everything that was planted would grow, and she said that of course it would, as long as it got proper water and the soil was good. So he undertook an experiment.

One week later, walking into the living room when his mother was screaming at the maids, insisting that they must have stolen the good crystal ware, he came clean and led them to one of the interior courtyards where they found all of the missing glasses buried under five inches of sandy soil.

He told her about the ocean, which she had only seen in pictures. The first time he took her and the kids to the coast, she was astounded by the sheer immensity and the loud noise of the crashing waves, many of which were more than ten feet tall. She had swum in ponds as a child and she had seen Lake Michigan while studying in college, but these had not prepared her for the Pacific Ocean. With some coaxing she waded in knee-deep and then yelped when she felt the rip tide pulling her strongly, as if intent on absconding with her to its watery depths.

He told her about seeing armadillos in the patio gardens, digging around and leaving piles of dirt on the cement which had to be swept back into place in the mornings. He told her about hot Christmas Eves spent at the beach and New Year's Eve with fireworks till dawn. The next day there would be brightly colored confetti and shredded newspaper and the red paper skins of firecrackers piled four inches deep in the streets.

Earthquakes, he warned her, were fairly common. You had to be sure to scramble under a table or stand in a doorway if you felt the earth trembling beneath you. That was a frightening thought, and she tried hard to imagine what that would feel like. She worried that she would miss it, or, like a fun-house ride, it would topple her so completely that she wouldn't be able to get under a table.

Then there were the rains. The fact that she could practically set her watch by the time of day that it rained, every day during the rainy season, never ceased to amaze her. The weather had never behaved like that in Illinois. And when a tropical storm blew in and it rained incessantly for several days, she suddenly understood why all of the houses had tiled floors, tiled kickboards going up four inches along the wall, and large drains in all of the interior patios. She also could see why even the small houses had several patios.

Tall, thick cement walls, almost three times her height, separated one house from the next in the modest neighborhood where they lived in Cuscatlán, which was called a *colonia*. After they had been in the house only a few weeks, she was shocked to find that Rodrigo had been saving up glass bottles so he could pay a laborer to cement the broken shards along the top edges.

"It's to keep us safe," he said, blushing slightly. "It's just that we are considered very wealthy here."

Laura nodded. She had seen that over 90% of the population were poorer than she'd ever dreamed people could be, even the tiny middle class, like herself and the family, were envied.

She was not happy about the fact that her husband had to hire a *sereno*, a night watch guard who carried a machete and patrolled outside the house while the family slept, but Rodrigo explained that sometimes it was these very same *serenos* who would, if families refused to pay, break into the houses. Or tip a robber off if they knew that no one was home. Of course, none of this was verifiable, and since police were also easily bribed, the best thing to do when a *sereno* offered to guard your house was to pay him, thank him and shut up.

After having spent her life seeing only soberly colored houses and buildings, in shades of cream or gray, the bright blues, yellows, oranges and pinks of the walls were a shock. So

174

were the dozens of new fruits she saw in the noisy markets, and the vivid yellows and pinks of flowering trees with their highly contrasting dark trunks. There were birds, like the ubiquitous green *pericos*, which flew in large, noisy, gregarious flocks and which didn't even have a name in English. And, although Rodrigo had told her that there were only two seasons, she was still surprised to live in a land where it was warm or hot all year long. She could wear skirts and sandals even in January.

However, there were things about living in El Salvador that deeply saddened her. When they travelled by highway at night, out in the country, she would look out the window and see men so skinny that their ribs showed through their thin shirts, squatting on their haunches around fires. And then there were the women, her age and older, whom she passed every day. They carried immense, heavy baskets on their heads, their backs erect. Looking into their faces she saw that they were only wisps of their former selves, hollowed out with tiredness, disease and sadness. Their mouths were pocked with black holes where there should have been teeth and their thin, sucked-dry breasts hung dejectedly under their brown dresses. And then there were the children with big, beautiful brown eyes, dirty faces and matted hair, pulling on her sleeve and begging for food.

As a matter of fact, Laura realized that she had never seen so many people before in her life. There were literally people everywhere. There was nowhere she could look that she didn't see someone. Even when they were out in the country, driving past fields and looking toward the mountains, there was always another human being visible. Illinois was not like that.

She had not had an easy childhood, but she felt like she had lived the life of royalty compared to the squalor in which practically everyone in the country lived. Everyone, that is, except for the few wealthy people. Too many of the well-off people, she observed to her disgust, treated the poor as if they were vermin, as if they had contracted some filthy disease which

175

could easily be transmitted to them were they to even look upon them, let alone treat them with any dignity.

Not all of the wealthy people were like this, it's true. In the three and a half years that she lived in that country she did meet kind, hard-working wealthy people who treated their servants well and who ran organizations that helped the poor. But, unfortunately, these people were not the norm.

Rodrigo's family owned land in one of the far-away provinces, and her visits with them were infrequent. On certain occasions, such as a special birthday or holiday, Rodrigo took her and the children to their city, driving for hours on narrow, winding roads that trekked up and down and around the mountains. But mostly there was little contact between the families.

Laura knew that her husband was very loyal to the memory of his father, who had passed away while he was in high school in the capital city, but his mother had re-married and Rodrigo felt very uncomfortable with the new situation. His brother had moved to Mexico City just two years earlier, and his sister lived in Florida. So living in El Salvador left Rodrigo and Laura in a small vacuum, absent of family. Neither was overly bothered with that.

Rodrigo had good friends in the city, chiefly Adelmo, whose wedding Rodrigo had attended during the Christmas break of 1961. The two friends had corresponded regularly throughout the years and Laura welcomed Adelmo like a brother to her husband. Adelmo worked at the University, helped him to get a job there. Adelmo and his wife, Adel (her full name was Adelgonda, but that was too long for Laura) were frequent visitors at their house and vice versa. At first, Laura's Spanish was painfully inadequate and other than smiling and nodding and offering Adel something else to drink, it was slow going, but with time, Laura learned more Spanish and things improved.

176

One point of contention between Rodrigo and Laura in this new environment was the idea of having a live-in maid. Rodrigo wanted to get one and Laura did not. She insisted that she had always worked hard, both growing up and in their small apartment in Chicago, and there was no reason for her not to continue doing so now.

Every few months they would have a similar conversation. "Don't you think it's time we got someone to help you out in the house?" he would ask.

She guessed there was probably an element of peer pressure as well since everyone they knew had maids. But Laura would shake her head and change the subject.

It was being all alone in the house all day, especially once the children started attending kindergarten, that finally wore her down.

"But I don't want a maid," she insisted when she finally agreed that they could hire someone. "Just a cook."

Once she gave in, the idea of having someone who could go to the market with her and teach her how to prepare the strange foods that people ate, was enticing. Rodrigo put the sign up on the window of the garage door but Laura was convinced that it would take weeks, if not months, to find someone suitable, so she put it out of her mind.

The very next day someone knocked at the door. She was a small-framed woman with delicate features and Laura's first impression was that she looked like a shorter version of Olive Oil, black hair bundled into a bun, fairly flat chested and practically no waist.

People regularly knocked at the door, offering to sell fresh, hot tortillas, *pupusas*, tamales, mangoes, and a myriad of other things, so Laura assumed that this lady was also a vendor. She greeted her in the few words of Spanish that she could say, but the woman looked slightly puzzled. Then she pointed to sign in the garage and simultaneously, Laura realized that the woman was not carrying a basket of things. She was applying for the job!

"Oh, thank you for stopping by," said Laura, forgetting, as she often did in moments when she got nervous, that people could not understand her. She was instantly embarrassed and said, without thinking, "Oh, dear me, I'm sure you can't understand me, can you?"

The woman, who was about her age, looked at her, studying her carefully as if trying to figure her out. It was a look that Laura got often.

"Has no one here ever seen a foreigner?" Laura had asked her husband. It seemed like everyone she met was thoroughly perplexed by her. They might give her an odd look when they first saw her, but as soon as they realized that she couldn't understand what they were trying to say, most people were at a loss. If Rodrigo was nearby, the person would instinctively turn to him and ask him to translate, but if she was alone, people would shy away and quickly give up trying to reach her.

Laura half expected this woman standing at her door to do the same, and she was already making a mental note that she would have to ask Rodrigo to teach her some phrases to help her deal with this new situation. Why hadn't she thought of that before?

Then the woman did something so unexpected and so sweet that Laura was immediately drawn to her. Without skipping a beat, she mimed stirring a pot and peeling some vegetables. Laura realized that the woman had not understood that Laura knew what she was there for. And she was engaging her! A smile broke over Laura's face. She realized that this was a woman she could feel comfortable with. Laura was just beginning to wonder how she would tell her to come back later, when her husband was home, when the woman mimed something else. A baby. She was also a mother.

Oh. Well, that would explain why she was resourceful and had so quickly found a way to communicate. But did Laura want a live-in maid (Rodrigo had explained that most maids were live-in) who brought another child? It was a scenario she had not considered. She thought quickly.

"How big is she?" Laura asked, complementing her words with gestures.

The woman placed her hand like she was telling Laura to stop, palm outward, but from her gestures Laura could tell that she was demonstrating that her child was about as big as Rodrigo Junior and Isabella. Laura considered. It wasn't necessarily a bad thing, was it? The woman could bring her child and then Laura's children would have someone to play with. All at once she felt all her former hesitancy toward having someone else in the house with her melt away.

"Yes, that would be perfectly fine," she said, nodding vigorously and reaching out to give her new friend a hug.

After she closed the door, Laura practically skipped to the kitchen. "Time to make a pumpkin pie," she said to herself. It was Rodrigo's favorite dessert and she was sure that he would be pleased that she had finally found someone to work in the house with her.

179

Chapter 28

El Salvador, 1969

Sesi

Working at *Doña* Laura's place was very different from working anywhere else I had ever been. For one thing, there were no other maids in the house, which at first I thought was really strange. I was a little afraid that I would not be able to handle all of the work because at *Doña* Flor Maria's house, which was not large or grand, there had been two of us *muchachas* working for just two people and it's not like we had a lot of extra time on our hands. But I wanted the job so badly, and was loving every minute of being able to be with Rocio all the time, that I was willing to do whatever it took to keep the job.

What made it bearable was the surreal fact that *Doña* Laura did the housework with me. It was so completely unlike anything I'd ever known. I mean, people get *muchachas* so they don't have to do anything at all. They can fix their hair and go visit with friends, go shopping, or simply sit around and read magazines. They don't help with laundry or work in the kitchen or pick up stuff that the kids leave around. They don't sweep or mop or even make their own cup of coffee.

But *Doña* Laura did all of these things. It was like she was playing the game with a different set of rules when I had never dreamed that other rules could exist. At first I was completely against it, insisting that she sit down while I got her coffee, and practically wrestling the broom away from her. I was afraid that she was doing it to show me that I wasn't working fast enough or hard enough and she wanted to show me how to do it.

I was wrong, however. It wasn't that she was disappointed in me.

"I'm used to doing these things," she said to me. Yes, maybe not in those exact words, but that's what she said. "I feel bad sitting around while you do all the work."

Let me tell you, I could only think that people up north were different both on the outside and on the inside as well. It was an eye-opening experience.

The other thing that really shocked me and that took me a while to get used to was the fact that she treated me as if I was her complete equal. For instance, a few months into my work at her house, I let it be known that I was not exactly crazy about cooking. I know, you are probably shaking your wrist at me right now, slapping your fingers together at my insolence since, after all, I was hired to be a cook.

But, again, *Doña* Laura was different. Instead of being insulted or disgruntled by my revelation, she took it in stride.

"If you will teach me how to cook some basics like rice and beans, fried plantains and green rice, then we can share the cooking."

And so that's what we did. I taught her how to sort through the rice and wash it thoroughly before cooking it. I showed her how to make tamales and the best way to toast the thick, Salvadoran tortillas. At the market, we bought plump yellow plantains and I showed her how to wrap them in newspaper to ripen. When they were ready, skins nice and black and thin, I showed her how to peel them and slice them in broad slabs, then fry them until they were soft and golden. After

181

draining them, we would sprinkle them with sugar.

I also taught her to cut green, hard bananas in thin slices and fry them to make chips. And I showed her the other bananas that grew here—reddish orange ones that were very sweet, and tiny ones, like fingers, that took a long time to ripen.

Once she knew enough, we took turns cooking. I would fix the mid-day meal, which was the largest, and she would fix dinner. Or we would take turns by days of the week. And often we would work together in the kitchen, which was nice too.

Plus, she taught me how to make some of the pastries that she liked to bake. I must say, if you have never had a pastry from gringo-land, you haven't lived. *Doña* Laura made all kinds of fruit pies that would melt in your mouth and cakes that were white and fluffy or a dark, chocolaty heaven. But the most surprising and delicious things she made, hands down, were what she called donus. They were shaped like little circles, but they were missing their centers. They were kind of like bread— you had to let them rise—but then you fried them and dipped them in sugar. Absolute heaven!

As you can probably imagine, it took me and *Doña* Laura a bit of time to get to know each other. At first she didn't speak much Spanish at all so we mostly communicated with sign language. She blushed a lot, and let me tell you, it was something else to see her chele skin turn as red as a ripened mango. I could tell that she was embarrassed not to be able to talk to me. But I didn't mind. I found it interesting and challenging, like going to school and learning something new. And I didn't want her to feel bad that she couldn't understand me so I talked to her like I had spoken to Rocio, when she was a baby.

"¿Tienes sed?" I would say, miming drinking a glass of water and then pointing to her. She would nod, and then I would tell her how to say that yes, she was thirsty.

One time, right around lunch time, she said to me, "*Tengo hombre.*" It was funny because she meant to say "*Tengo hambre,*" which means "I'm hungry," but instead she had said that she had a man! I chuckled and grabbed little Rodrigo, who was riding around the house on his tricycle, and I said "*Sí, tienes un hombre y también tienes hambre,*" pointing first to him and then to her stomach. She realized what she had said and slapped her forehead and we both giggled.

It's funny, *Doña* Laura and I could hardly speak to each other, but we had so much to say. She had this little green book with a cloth cover and gold lettering that she would use when she wanted to say a particular word, like a kind of fruit or a certain object. The book had the words in her strange language and then in regular Spanish. When we would get stuck on a point that was important, but that I just couldn't understand even with her mimes, she would page through the book and then point her finger to a word and suddenly it would all make sense to me. After a few times, she showed me how to use the book too and I could find regular words that had her unpronounceable words next to them.

But sometimes, even her book said words that didn't make any sense. For instance, when she talked to me about snow, she found the word, "*nieve,*" but I still didn't know what it meant. Ever resourceful, she got up and went to the refrigerator, opened the freezer, and took out some of the tiny white ice that formed on the walls.

"*Nieve,*" she said.

I nodded. I had always thought of that as "ice," but "snow" was a good word too.

Then she pointed up and said that it fell from the sky, and as I've mentioned earlier, I did not really believe her. I wasn't trying to be rude or anything, but she was miming that the ice-snow came from the clouds—she even drew little pictures of

183

them—and I knew that ice only came from machines.

"There's so much snow that falls that the whole world turns white," she said.

I stared at her.

"It can get deep, too," she said, pointing to her thighs.

It was pure nonsense and I didn't think that it was the fault of the little green book. I continued watching her, trying to keep a straight face.

"You don't believe me?"

I really did not wish to offend her—she was a terrific story-teller and as you know, I really respect good stories and their tellers.

"If there was that much snow, everything would die," I challenged.

"It does. I mean, many of the birds fly south. Other animals dig holes and sleep. And the trees lose all of their leaves."

There were so many problems with her explanation that it was hard to know where to start. How on earth would birds "know" that it was time to fly away? And once they left that cold land, what would ever entice them to return if it was just going to get cold again in a few months? Did she expect me to believe that they would just keep going back and forth like that? Either our birds were much smarter, or she was fibbing.

And as for animals digging holes, sure, some animals might, but the sloth up in the trees, he was surely not going to dig holes. And even if he did, what then? He would crawl inside and go to sleep for months on end? How would he even have enough air to breathe if there was snow piled thigh-deep on top of the ground? I mean, really, how gullible did she think I was?

But it was the tree argument that really tipped me off to

her tall tales. I mean, how would all of the trees, who have even less of a chance of communicating with one another than birds or animals, know that it was suddenly time to lose all of their leaves at once, keep them off the entire time it was cold and then grow them all back again when the snow went away? And, how would they know to keep repeating the process every few months? Our trees down here never did that and it was hard to imagine that trees would be that different. Furthermore, what would people do for food if there were no fruit trees or plants growing for months on end while the world turned into a giant freezer? Everyone would die!

But I let her have her fun, drawing pictures of beautiful six-pointed stars that she said were individual snowflakes.

"No two are alike," she added.

I tell you, she was a great storyteller, all those details! We had so much to chatter about that time flew by and the work got done and I was having fun, real fun, for the first time in my life. It was almost better than those days of lovely walks in the park with Figo. Different, certainly, but yes, in many ways better because I felt more grounded and more certain of the future. The worst had happened and I had survived.

My little Rocio played with *Doña* Laura's children and soon she was saying strange words in their language and they were finally learning to speak intelligibly. In the mornings, I walked them to their private school, and then went with Rocio to her public school, just down the road. In the afternoon I would collect them all, bring them back to the house and *Doña* Laura would have afternoon snacks prepared for all three of them and they would sit together at the table to eat.

One day, I remember, *Doña* Laura asked me about crocodiles. I'm not sure how we got on the subject—we must have been talking about rivers or something—and she said that she had never seen a crocodile and would not know what to do if

185

she did. Here in El Salvador, teaching our children how to run away from crocodiles is one of the first things we do when they are raised in the villages. Crocodiles are opportunists, in most cases, and they'll go after the little ones with no hesitation or compunction.

"The trick is," I told her confidently, "that you don't run in a straight line. You have to run in a zig-zag. That's because even though crocodiles are water animals, they can still run pretty fast in a straight line to catch their prey on land. But if you run in a zig-zag, it confuses them and they can't catch you." It's an important thing to learn. I had learned that many predators were that way too—even two-legged ones. If you ran straight away, they would catch you, but if you found a way to run that confused them, then you could get away. I didn't tell her that part, but I think she understood.

And in any case, I was glad to be teaching her something that she could teach her children too. The world is a dangerous place, even in areas where you wouldn't necessarily expect it, like rivers. They provide our water for living, but they can be hazardous if you're not careful. So, it's good to know these things and not just fill your mind with stories about pieces of clouds falling down from the sky and turning the whole world white.

Chapter 29

El Salvador, 1970

Sesi

"Are the people up there in those airplanes just like us?" I asked *Doña* Laura as we were hanging up some clothes to dry on the lines one day. I had been working at her house for over a year and her Spanish was much better. And I had just noticed the tiny white dot making its way across the azure surface of the sky, like a little snail, leaving a furry trail as it went. I had seen airplanes do this before, and I had heard the rumor that those tiny dots, not much bigger than stars, were really large enough to hold people when they were on the ground. But I wasn't quite sure I believed it.

For one thing, there was no way a person could be small enough to fit inside one. For another, I had never seen an airplane down on the ground. I had not seen a star or the moon on the ground either, though, so that much did not surprise me.

It was a question that I had pondered over the years, but as I was certain that none of my peers knew the answer either, I figured it was just one more thing I would go to the grave without knowing. You see, it wasn't a question that a *muchacha* could ask the person for whom she worked. Most people did not take well to having inquisitive *muchachas*. I wished that I had asked Figo, as he certainly would have known the answer since he was in the university, but I didn't think of it at the time, and then I lost my chance.

Doña Laura looked at me and laughed and I immediately felt ashamed. What a silly question I had asked! Of course those people were different. I should have known. I should never have believed those *muchachas* at that last house where I worked who said that they knew for a fact that their employers had ridden in airplanes. I had been taken for a fool and now *Doña* Laura would think worse of me. I turned my face away so that she would not see my embarrassment.

"Sesi, of course those are the same kind of people up there," she said. I turned back to look at her, just to be sure that she wasn't teasing me, and I was shocked to the marrow by the certainty on her face. Then she said something even more surprising, but you've probably already guessed it: she told me that she, herself, had ridden in an airplane. I was so stunned to hear that she had been that high up in the air that I had to feign going to the bathroom so I could be alone to think about that.

When I came back, full of questions, that's when she explained how her country was so far away and that was how she had come to El Salvador. Of course, that meant that her children had also ridden in the airplane. And *Don* Rodrigo Manuel. It was shocking that so many people had been up so high, above the clouds, for several hours.

That gave me a lot to think about so I just listened quietly. She said that it was basically like a bus with wings, only a bit bigger. And the wings didn't flap. She said that being up so high is what made the airplane look small, but that when it came down, it was really quite big. She even opened one of her books and showed me a picture of one.

So I know she was telling me the truth, even if it was hard to really believe her. She said that there was a place where all the planes landed and it's like a big open field with a few roads that cars don't drive on because these are for the planes to come and go on. She said the planes are really noisy, but on the inside you can't hardly hear the noise.

One day, before I die, I would like to go to this place and look at those airplanes with my own eyes. And maybe, while I'm at it, I'll ride on one and go to see the country where she comes from, full of really pale people and ice clouds that break off in little chunks and fall down, softer than rain. That would be a sight to see.

Another day as *Doña* Laura worked alongside me companionably sorting through the dried beans and rice, she asked me, "You're not from San Salvador?"

"No, I'm from a town close to Santa Ana."

"Oh," she said after a pause. "I've never been there."

"Well, it's like any other town, I guess. Like any other one I saw on my way here to the capital city."

"Why did you come to San Salvador?" she asked.

"I was twelve years old when I found out that my mother's neighbor's daughter, a girl named Linda, had come to the capital and made a lot of money working here." Then I told her about how proud her mother had been that Linda sent home lots of money and how my mother dreamed that I would do the same thing, working in a big house and wearing fancy uniforms. "I imagined that once I reached this city I would never run out of work.

"I see. And have you found Linda, now that you're here? Is the house where she works as grand as you thought it would be?"

This made me blush.

"I did find out where she worked," I confessed, not

meeting her eyes, "but I decided not to do that myself."

I swallowed and she waited for me to finish.

"It turns out that she is in a brothel."

That made both of us feel very warm and a little uncomfortable, so we giggled.

"No wonder she made so much money," she said.

"I know. My mother asked me that same question too, but I never told her what Linda does, so she just thinks I'm lazy."

"Mothers can be hard to please," she agreed. "My mother was never happy with anything I did."

Then she told me about her life on the farm. I was completely dumbfounded as our conversations, strung together over many days, picking our way slowly through new vocabulary words, led to us stepping barefoot on the painfully sharp stones of bad memories. She told me about her mother's neglect.

"She was always so tired and so angry. I had the feeling that my brothers and sister and I annoyed her by simply being alive and living in her house. No matter how hard I tried, how well I did all of the chores, nothing made her happy."

After that, *Doña* Laura went on to tell me about her father's inappropriate behavior.

"I never really told anyone about the terrible things he did, and except for Sally, I'm not sure if anyone ever knew."

I understood what she meant. It was embarrassing to speak of men's ill behavior. It was also surprising to realize how universal men's bad actions were. I had never really thought about it, but now that I did, it made sense. Dogs of all colors and shapes still barked and bit you if they were mad. People were the same.

190

It made me really feel bad for her when I heard how persistent her father was, insinuating himself on her progressively over the years. I imagined her like Sara, so innocent and full of life, and I wished I could go into her past life and somehow stop him from hurting her. Then I was biting my nails with worry when I heard about him attacking her that night out by the chicken coop, and I cheered when she told me about how she threatened to shoot him if he touched her again.

Her stories made it possible for me to tell her mine. "*Don* Enrique tried to force himself on me once," I said, and then went on to describe what had happened that night after I put Sara to bed. It was one of those things that I had pushed completely out of my mind and I was surprised by the emotion I felt as I remembered the details and put them into words.

I also told her how he had abused poor little Blanca. As I spoke of him I realized that in my mind I had formed an alliance with her and I knew that if I ever met her, I would be extra nice to her.

Then I told her about running away and how much Miranda helped me.

"You were so brave, sleeping outdoors. That first night in the bamboo patch, how scary!"

And would you believe it, talking to *Doña* Laura and seeing her reaction made me cry about that night, for the first time. I had been distressed and had done what was needed to be done. I had been worried and frightened, but I guess I had turned it all into a story, like it was happening to someone else and I was just telling it. But telling her made me realize that I had never cried about that night.

Somehow, seeing the events from that night through her eyes changed things for me. I got up from the table where we were sitting, having a cup of tea from equal mugs, and went and washed my face. Afterwards, it was the strangest thing, but I

191

somehow felt stronger and, I don't know how else to describe it, but somehow I felt cleaner on the inside after telling her.

She also told me about her younger sister, whom she missed very much.

"I wish we had a telephone in the house so I could call Sally and hear her voice," she told me. I had no sister, but if I had, I probably would have wanted to call her too.

"Your sister must be very wealthy to have a phone," I offered. I knew that telephones were very expensive and only people like *Don* Adelmo and *Doña* Adelgonda could afford to have them installed.

"What? Oh, no, not at all. Telephones are very common in the US," she said. "Practically everyone has one in their home."

And that made me wonder, yet again, what it must have been like to live there, up north, with clouds that freeze and break into pieces and fall down, still cold, and everyone with telephones in their houses. She had given up a lot to come live here in El Salvador.

We continued sharing like that, over the coming months, as we folded clothes or took walks to the market together or cooked dinner. I told her more about Sara and her picky ways and her endearing love. I described what it was like to walk in the countryside by day and find a place to sleep, hidden from people and wild animals, at night. I described my love story with Figo and his tragic end. We were both crying when I finished that story.

Then I told her about my hunting for jobs and she got a kick out of the story of how one astute old woman "interviewed" applicants for the position of a *muchacha* by first giving them a test. She would place the girl in a bedroom and ask her to clean it from top to bottom. Then she would close the door and walk away.

That part was pretty normal, but the trick was that under the bed, right in the center, the old woman would have placed a ten centavo coin. Those were the smallest, flattest ones. After the *muchacha* declared that she had finished cleaning the room, the older woman would go back into the bedroom by herself and close the door behind her. She would take her time inspecting everything, checking to see that the floor was spotless and that even the kickboards were dusted and that all of the pillows were fluffed and that the edges of the bedspread hung evenly on either side. Then she would look under the bed to see if the ten centavo coin was still there.

If it was, it meant that the *muchacha* was lazy and didn't sweep completely under the bed, so she wouldn't hire her. If it was gone, then she would know that the *muchacha* was a thief. The only way anyone got a job in that household was if they did a great job cleaning and if they handed her the ten centavos as soon as they called the old woman in to inspect their work.

When her Spanish got even better, I told *Doña* Laura the Monkey Princess story, of course, and as many other tales as I could remember or make up.

Doña Laura also told me wonderful stories. She talked about movies, which I had only been to once, and about people landing on the moon, which I didn't really completely believe. That was even more strange than the airplane story or the clouds made out of ice that managed to stay in the sky.

"In my country, everyone speaks like I do, in English," she told me. "As a matter of fact, before I met Rodrigo, I had never met anyone who spoke Spanish."

She even taught me a few words in English, which my lazy tongue found hard to imitate. She taught me to say "jes" when I agreed with something and "gooth morneeng" when I first saw her in the morning. It felt really funny to say those

193

things, but I also felt proud at the same time.

I showed her the pleasure of eating green, hard mangoes mixed with cucumbers and smothered with lemon juice and salt for breakfast. She taught me how to make pastries and pie crusts and donus, those wonderful delights which, as I mentioned earlier, were my favorite.

When *Doña* Laura laughed, her whole being laughed too, not just her mouth. And when she was sad, it was like the lights in the room had gone out. She got down on her hands and knees and played with the children—all three of them—and at dinner she invited me and Rocio to share the table with her family. I admired her deeply for finding a way to leave the misery of her childhood behind her and forge a new path that was paved with the love and acceptance of those who were different from her.

She embraced life fully and I found that I wanted to emulate her. She didn't just want to stay alive, she wanted to make a difference. She wanted to make the world a better place, even if it was in some small way, like teaching me new skills that I could use in my life afterwards. And for all these reasons I will forever be grateful to the Virgin Mary for putting *Doña* Laura into my life for those few years.

Chapter 30

El Salvador, 1971

Laura

Laura woke up feeling nauseous. Her first thought was to try to remember what she had eaten the day before. Since moving to El Salvador over a year ago this was an unfortunate routine to which she had become accustomed. Her American stomach was beginning to become hardened to the new food, but there were still times when she would have something that just didn't agree with her. On a few occasions, she had been reduced to having liquids and white rice and boiled chicken until her stomach recovered, but most of the time she could just take it easy for a few days and then she was fine again.

She lay still for several moments, her hands cupping her stomach, willing herself to feel better. But herself was having none of it. What had set her off this time? They had eaten at Adel's house and she had served...no, that was two nights ago. Yesterday they ate at home. She bought a fish at the market and Sesi had shown her how to prepare it. Could the fish have been bad? Just thinking about the fish made her stomach flip and she raced out of bed, toward the toilet.

After rinsing her mouth with some cold water, she realized that she still felt queasy. She splashed her face and neck and then it suddenly occurred to her that the children might be ill too. She grabbed a robe and headed barefoot down the hall to check on them. Both were feeling fine. And her husband was still sleeping soundly. Well, Saturday mornings were meant for sleeping in. She considered going back to bed, but more than anything, she felt like she wanted to eat something salty. Crackers. Yes, crackers were her go-to food when she was queasy those mornings when she was expecting the twins...

Shit! It could only mean one thing. She went back into the bedroom and found the calendar hanging from a bleak nail on the wall. It was one of those calendars that the banks gave away at Christmas each year, with beautiful aerial pictures of different parts of El Salvador. Her eyes passed swiftly over the majestically tall trees, laden with pink blossoms, reflected in a lake. She scanned the white blocks of this month's days quickly, looking for the penciled-in "G". George was what her freshman roommates had called their periods. "George is here again," or "George is late," or "George is being a complete jerk," were an easy, embarrassment-free way to talk about their cycles without inciting unwanted interest from eavesdroppers.

Her periods had been fairly regular before the twins were born, but afterwards, they had become more erratic. Sometimes they came as frequently as every two weeks, other times they stretched out to five weeks. When she first moved to El Salvador her period had been delayed and she had panicked, but it had come, six whole weeks after the last one. It was this event that prompted her to record her cycle start date by marking an inconspicuous little "G" on the calendar.

Birth control was something she had initially balked at. She had been raised Catholic, after all, and she loved children. But her pregnancy with the twins had not been easy. Perhaps no pregnancy with twins was easy. And after she gave birth, her doctor said that her uterus was scarred. He had strongly suggested that she have a hysterectomy, but Laura had refused. She thought that maybe someday she would like to try again.

196

And most likely, she would not carry twins again and it would be all right.

Then the doctor had insisted that she start taking the pill and wait six or seven years before attempting another pregnancy. She had been disappointed, but her long recovery after their birth and the assault to her being that resulted from being the sole caretaker of two newborns had softened her regret. In the end, she had agreed to go on the pill.

She ran her finger up the page through the rows of weeks, then, her heart racing, reached up to the nail and unhooked the page for the previous month. There was the G, right on the top line. Shit! She felt so conflicted. It was too soon to be pregnant again. The kids were still too little.

No, they were already five years old. It was a good time for a sibling.

But, she wasn't sure that she really wanted another baby after all. At least, not now. Not here, where she couldn't speak to the doctors.

But a baby! That would be nice! Rodrigo would be so happy.

But maybe she wasn't pregnant. She was jumping to conclusions before she had the facts. Why did she play these games with herself?

Her stomach spun again and she placed her hand on the wall to steady herself. Her other hand still grasped the calendar page gingerly by the edge. She had planned to use these brightly colored pictures to decorate the children's room at the end of the year, cutting off the edges with advertisements and either gluing them to a piece of poster board, or maybe framing each one individually. She still hadn't decided but she had been so careful not to mess up the pages.

She took a deep breath and then carefully counted the

lines of weeks between the last recorded "G" and today's date. Seven. That meant that her period was at least three weeks late. And she was nauseous. And no one else in the house was sick. She carefully hooked the page back over the nail and went back to the bathroom to heave some more.

Chapter 31

El Salvador, 1971

Sesi

I was not that surprised when *Doña* Laura told me that she was pregnant. When you work for (and with) someone every day, you kind of get a feel for what's normal, and what isn't. Even though she was chele, which made her a bit harder to read, the last couple of weeks I had noticed dark circles under her eyes. And when we went to the market, she was more fussy than usual about what to buy. I remembered from being pregnant with Rocio that my sense of smell was the first thing to go crazy and become so sensitive that I suddenly couldn't stand things that I had never paid that much attention to before. This was even before my tummy started stretching and Figo asked me to marry him. I had even begun taking an aversion to his smell, come to think of it, though it would not have been enough to keep me away from him.

But, we were talking about *Doña* Laura. When she told me about expecting a baby, I was happy for her. She was so excited and was talking about her new baby a lot. She told me that at first she wasn't sure if she wanted a baby, but now she was thrilled that the twins would have a new baby brother (she was convinced it would be a boy) and she was making plans about the crib and how the twins room would be re-arranged.

I listened to her, but part of me, a very selfish and ugly part of me, I'm ashamed to admit, was unhappy about the situation. I've told you I'm going to be honest in this story so I'll explain to the best of my ability. It wasn't that I was jealous of her for having a husband. *Don* Rodrigo Manuel reacted the same way my dear Figo had reacted when he found out I was pregnant—he was attentive to *Doña* Laura and protective and gentle and kind. You could see that he was happy to be having another baby.

I would have had a husband like that too if the Virgin Mary had thought that I could not handle life without him. I had finally accepted that.

But even after all the gentleness and kindness that *Doña* Laura had shown me, I was not as kind as I should have been. I guess you could say that my heart was as black as a cricket's heart. You see, I was stupidly unhappy because I was only thinking of myself and my work. I had gotten spoiled, you could say, having *Doña* Laura there by my side, keeping me company at the market and cooking and cleaning. And I knew, I just knew, that as her pregnancy progressed, she would feel less inclined to do these things. I also knew it would be a lot of work to take care of the new baby, especially with two other children around, (three if you count Rocio.)

I didn't fear having to work harder—that has never frightened me—but I did fear that *Don* Rodrigo Manuel would convince *Doña* Laura to hire another woman in the house and that our lovely friendship would be shattered permanently with the addition of these two people, one brand new and one older and given to her own (and in my mind, stubborn) ways.

This is why I still blame myself for what happened afterwards. When I realized that I was having these awful, selfish thoughts, I should have immediately taken an offering to the

Virgin and asked her to forgive me and to bless *Doña* Laura and the new baby. I knew that that was the customary thing to do. But I found reasons to be busy and "forget" to do it. When I'm feeling more generous with myself I like to believe that I was still planning to do it at some point, before the baby was born. But the awful truth of the matter is that I dallied too long and then it was too late because something terrible happened.

It was a Tuesday morning and *Don* Rodrigo Manuel had gone in early to the University. I had taken the children to school and then washed up the dishes. I was waiting for *Doña* Laura to come downstairs, but by that time she was about five months with child, and her morning sickness was still so bad that she usually took longer in the mornings. I wasn't particularly worried about her so I kept cleaning things around the house, you know, things that sometimes you don't get around to doing as frequently as you'd like. I mopped the kitchen floor and then dried it on my hands and knees. The kitchen usually dried pretty quickly anyway, but I didn't want to take a chance that *Doña* Laura would come down and slip, in her state.

Then I dusted the living room and started the beans boiling for dinner. At about noon I began to worry that she had not come down and had anything to eat yet. So I prepared her a tray, something she never liked me to do, which is why I had waited so long to do it in the first place, and I took it to her room. I remember I was holding it carefully as I had over-filled the coffee cup and I didn't want it to spill onto the toasted bread. I balanced the tray between my hip and the wall, steadying it with one hand so I could knock with the other. There was no answer.

I knocked again. Still no answer.

I stood there biting my lip and wondering what to do for a few more seconds, and then I decided to risk her anger—not that she was regularly angry, but I thought she might be upset if I was waking her up—to be sure that she was okay.

201

I dropped the tray and let out a little scream when I saw her. The bed linens were white, but the center, where she lay, was a deep crimson color. Her face was paler than a ghost's and she was sweating and gritting her teeth in pain. I ran to her, feeling completely helpless, calling her name and chattering so fast that there was no way she could have understood what I said.

"Sesi," she said in a soft moan, and returned to gritting her teeth.

"I'll be right back, *Doña* Laura," I said, slowly so she could understand me. Then I took off running as fast as I could.

I ran to *Doña* Adelgonda's house, which was only a block away, thankfully. I cannot tell you about my run, if I passed anyone I knew or if my sandals echoed hollowly on the scalding pavement. It was all a blur as I worried that *Doña* Laura was going to die.

I also don't remember *Doña* Adelgonda's maid answering the door, though it must have been her, or the frantic message I communicated. The first clear memory I have is her picking up the phone, which I had rarely ever seen someone using. She made two calls: one for an ambulance and the other to *Don* Rodrigo Manuel at the University. He was in class so she left a message with the Dean's secretary. Then she ran back to the house with me, and up the steps to *Doña* Laura's room.

"She's having a miscarriage, you're right," *Doña* Adelgonda confirmed when she saw her friend. She tried to get her to sit up and take some liquid, but *Doña* Laura was delirious, speaking in English and closing her eyes.

"We have to get her ready to go," said *Doña* Adelgonda. "Let's get something for the blood."

I pulled out a fresh new sheet and we rolled it up and placed it between *Doña* Laura's legs. There was so much blood, it was very scary.

"Get some towels too," *Doña* Adelgonda told me. It was good that she was taking charge because I was so upset that it was hard to think straight. Then, between *Doña* Adelgonda and me, we helped *Doña* Laura to get up and go downstairs. I put more sheets on the couch and we made her comfortable there.

The men from the ambulance arrived shortly and put her on a stretcher and carried her out to the van. I rode in the ambulance with her—this was not customary, but *Doña* Laura held my hand tight and *Doña* Adelgonda explained to the men that *Doña* Laura was fond of me and that I should be allowed to keep her company as her mother did not live in the country. It was plain to everyone that *Doña* Laura was a foreigner even before she went back to mumbling things in English. I was so glad that *Doña* Adelgonda knew *Doña* Laura so well and could say these things so clearly.

I was frightened of going in the ambulance. "You ride with her, and I'll go home and get my car and meet you at the hospital," she told me. So I got inside the van and one of the men got in with us and the other one closed the doors.

It was a scary, long and bumpy ride to the hospital. The men had put a needle in *Doña* Laura's arm at the house and hooked her up to a bag with a long, plastic tube and some liquid coming out of it. I wanted to ask them what it was for, though I could guess that it was to help her, but I didn't dare speak to them lest they become angered and ask me to get out of the ambulance.

When we finally got to the hospital *Doña* Laura was moaning softly and the rolled up sheet between her legs was soaked through with blood. I jumped out of the van and the driver got into the back and, between the two of them, they lifted her out of the vehicle. I thought they would put her on a bed or in a wheelchair, but they didn't. They held her arms and helped her to walk into the hospital. I looked at her feet and felt really bad because I realized that between all of us, we had forgotten to put sandals on her, so she was walking barefoot.

I followed behind, trying to say comforting words to *Doña* Laura, who seemed really confused. The two men held her up, one on each side, and all she had to do was to keep moving forward. The sheet fell from between her legs, landing on the floor with a sickening splat, but we all just stepped around it, as if it was some particularly obscene dead thing that no one wanted to look at.

Doña Laura was muttering something and I stepped closer so I could hear what she was saying. To my relief, she spoke in Spanish. She was saying "*¿Dónde?*". She was asking where we were going. I told them her question and the men explained that the women's floor was not on the ground floor, but fortunately, the steps leading up to the maternity ward were right there, near the entrance.

I got close to her ear and spoke to her very gently, like I used to talk to Rocio when she was a baby and she got sick. I explained in simple terms, using slow, clear words, that we were going upstairs. She nodded and smiled weakly and I could feel my heart breaking in a million pieces.

We climbed the white, tiled steps very slowly. The stairwell was narrow so only one man could stand next to her and the other one was a step ahead, walking backwards and trying to support her as best he could. I came last, and near the top, I looked down and gasped as I saw the trail of *Doña* Laura's bloody footprints climbing up the cold tile steps.

We finally got to a room and they put her on a bed. Then the nurses asked me to step outside so they could change her out of her soiled gown and put her in a fresh one. As I was waiting outside, *Don* Rodrigo Manuel came running up. He had followed the trail of bloody footprints and he was as pale as a ghost. When he asked me how she was, all I could do was cry.

Luckily, a nurse came out and he was allowed to see his wife for a brief moment before she was taken into the operating room. *Doña* Adelgonda got there a few minutes later, and by this time there was someone mopping up the footprints and rinsing out the pink water.

We stayed for another hour, then it was time to pick up the children from school. *Doña* Adelgonda took me home and told me to change—I hadn't realized that I also had blood all over my dress from helping *Doña* Laura. I brought the kids home and made them a snack and told them stories until *Don* Rodrigo Manuel came home and said that *Doña* Laura was resting.

The next morning, after taking the children to school, I took flowers to the Virgin. I even spent the extra money I had been saving to buy some new pencils for Rocio, to be sure that I got an impressive bunch for the Virgin's altar. I knew that the baby would probably die, but I dearly wanted *Doña* Laura to live.

Doña Adelgonda told me that afternoon that *Doña* Laura had lost so much blood that she had needed a transfusion. *Doña* Adelgonda organized her friends and between them they were able to find a match for her blood type. Everyone gave blood, even *Don* Rodrigo Manuel and *Don* Abel. I volunteered to give blood too, which was a bit scary, though not painful. I would have done anything in my power to help in any way possible.

Don Miguel Eduardo was buried two days later at the cemetery by the church. We all dressed in our best clothes, and *Doña* Laura, still weak and paler than a sheet of paper, stood there without crying. Then we went back home and she stayed in bed for several weeks.

Don Rodrigo went back to work the following week and the house got very quiet. During the day I made soups for *Doña* Laura and took them to her room. She ate like a tiny bird, barely enough to sustain herself. At night, I took the kids in to see her, after their baths. When I wasn't taking care of her, I worked fervently on the house, praying with all my body for her full recovery. About ten days later, one afternoon when I walked into her bedroom carrying a tray with her broth, she asked if she could rather have some beef and potatoes. That's when I knew that the Virgin had at least partly forgiven me and that *Doña* Laura would be well again.

Chapter 32

El Salvador, 1971

Laura

After Laura lost her baby son, things changed for her. Or, better said, things changed inside of her. This was the closest she had ever come to fearing for her own life, and she had lost her baby's. She had lost all of her babies, as a matter of fact, because the doctor performed a tubal ligation while he was tending to her miscarriage. She only found this out later as the doctor only saw fit to inform her husband of this matter, after the fact.

"Her womb was in no condition to ever have another baby," he told Rodrigo. And that was the end of that.

For two weeks after she came home Laura stayed in bed. Her body was healing and her bruised heart was scabbing over, though it would take a lot longer to recover. When Rodrigo told her that she would never have any more babies, three days after she had come home, the day after the funeral, she spent the entire night crying big quiet tears laden with the sorrow of lost dreams, into her pillow. It was not that she had planned on having a big family. It was just that she was wholly unprepared to have the right to make that decision removed so completely and suddenly from her purview.

Seeing her children at night was the only thing that

207

brightened her days. But, as her body healed, her natural emotional resilience and love for life also crawled back. One morning she sat up to receive her lunch from Sesi and realized that it was too thin and watery for her new appetite. Sesi smiled and ran downstairs to fix her something else. Four days later, Laura got up and stepped carefully back into her life.

She and Sesi began taking walks in the middle of the day, before the rains came. Laura had gone out before she lost her baby on errands—to the market or a store or to the bank, but she had never just walked to see what things looked like. As her heart and body healed, she became more curious about her surroundings.

They walked from the busier streets to quieter neighborhoods. On one of these walks she heard a loud thonk. She looked around and saw nothing unusual, just houses and thick, green trees, some laden with fruit. There were cars and bikes and other people walking, but no one else seemed to have noticed the sound. They continued walking and then a few minutes later she heard another thonk.

"What's making that noise?" she asked Sesi.

"Mangoes."

"Mangoes?"

"They fall and hit the tin tiles on the roofs of the houses," Sesi explained, using her hands and pointing. Laura's Spanish, though much improved, still needed some help.

For some reason, the idea of big, ripe heavy mangoes falling off trees tickled Laura and she laughed openly for the first time since her baby's death. "Mangoes toppling from the sky!" she declared. "You don't believe me when I tell you about snow and hail falling from the sky," Laura said, "but you live in a place where it's perfectly normal for mangoes to fall from the sky!

Then she told Sesi how she had never tasted a mango before coming to El Salvador and how she thought they must be little gifts that the tree was offering. Sesi smiled too.

After this day, Laura began noticing flowering trees and plants that she had never seen before. The colors and shapes and variety were a constant surprise and delight. Sesi taught her the names of many of them. There were bright red hibiscus flowers with their long, yellow tongues sticking out. There were elegant orchids in many shades of pink. There were heliconias which looked like someone had doodled them into being, each part of the flower like a tear-drop that spilled precariously from the edge of the next slightly larger tear-drop. Some flowers were recognizable, like roses, but others were twists on varieties she knew from Illinois. There were irises that looked like butterflies and gladiolas of a wide range of colors.

There were also more butterflies than Laura had ever thought possible. There were tiny ones as small as her fingernail, and huge ones, whose wings were bigger than the palm of her hand and which looked like pieces of paper floating in the air. There were red ones and yellow ones and orange ones with green stripes and yellow dots. There were brown ones with red and white spots and impossibly light blue ones, outlined in black. For weeks she felt like she saw new butterfly patterns every time she looked.

They continued taking midday walks. Some days they went to parks, other days they went to sit quietly in a church. Still other days they strolled down larger streets where there were many shops. Then one day they walked to a bookstore near the American consulate and Laura found a book that was meant to help one learn Spanish on one's own. She flipped through the book, which was filled with cartoon characters engaged in different scenarios and mock conversations. There were phrases for use in almost all of the everyday situations she might encounter.

209

"This is just what I've been looking for," she told Sesi in her imperfect Spanish. Her dictionary and her workbooks had helped her limp along in Spanish, but she was sure this would give her Spanish a real boost.

She took home her treasure and studied it diligently, saying the words aloud and practicing every day with Sesi. If she was going to stay in this country for who knew how long, she wanted to be able to speak with everyone. Her children had already mastered Spanish fairly well and she was sure that with some practice, she could do it too.

One morning their walks took them past a shop that sold material. Laura knew how to sew and she had brought her sewing machine with her, but she had not yet used it.

"Let's get material for curtains," she said.

Sesi smiled and squeezed her hand.

Together they browsed for days, taking home swatches, holding them up to the windows and the walls.

"What do you think of this one?" Laura asked.

Sesi frowned in concentration. "Perhaps a little too dark?"

Laura nodded. "And this one has too much blue. I was thinking of something with more yellow."

Then Sesi held up another swatch. "This one looked different in the store than it does here."

Laura agreed. "Let's go to that other store we saw a few blocks past the bank."

It was so nice to have a project to look forward to! Finally, Laura made up her mind about the curtains and bought the material.

"Come, sit here by me and I'll show you how to sew on

a machine," she said. "This is how you make a bobbin," she said, pushing the spindle to one side. When she pressed the foot pedal, the little spool swirled, growing fat in the middle with the new thread.

"If you hold the thread over your finger, you can control where it goes and make the bobbin more even," Laura said.

Then she taught Sesi how to thread the machine, and finally, how to cut out the patterns and make curtains.

"My friend Miranda loved to sew," Sesi told her. "She would make the prettiest little flowers on dresses when they got holes in them."

"Do you keep in touch with her, now that you're here in San Salvador?" Laura asked.

Sesi nodded. "She is still in the village I told you about, at the house where she went when she left *Don* Enrique's house and I saw her there. One of my friends that I meet occasionally at the market has a cousin who lives in that village, so we send each other greetings that way. She knows I'm here."

"Well, if she's ever in town, I'd love to meet her," said Laura.

The curtains looked lovely in the living room. The two women smiled when they hung them.

"They look fabulous," Laura pronounced and Sesi heartily agreed.

Inspired by her success, Laura went back to the store and bought patterns. She made pretty dresses for the two little girls and a sailor outfit for her son who was obsessed with Popeye cartoons. Sesi beamed with joy. Then at Christmas, Laura surprised Sesi with some new dresses that she had sewn for her, and Sesi was so touched that she cried and gave Laura a big hug.

Laura also began baking regularly, experimenting with

the new fruits that she and Sesi bought at the market, and trying different combinations in her pies. Sometimes the fruits were a bit too tart and she learned to add more sugar. Other fruits were too insipid and she learned to add a tablespoon of lemon juice, squeezed fresh from the lemon tree that grew in front of her house and produced fruit all year.

When she made doughnuts, she was surprised to see how much everyone, especially Sesi, loved them.

"These are so good, you should really try selling them," said Adel when she was visiting one afternoon.

Laura did not need the money—it's not that she had ever considered herself wealthy, it was just that she felt like she had enough. But she knew that Sesi did need the money. Sesi had told her about wanting to save for Rocio's education, but the wages she made at Laura's house were not going to be enough, especially since she still sent money home to her mother.

"I have an idea, Sesi." Laura said the next day. "Why don't you try selling some doughnuts at the gates to the school, when you go pick up the children?"

Bake sales did well in the US, she reasoned, so they might work here as well. Sesi agreed that it was a good idea.

They spent the morning baking, and then Sesi left early that afternoon to pick up the kids, bearing a tray of warm, delicious treats. She charged twenty-five centavos for each one, and came home with an empty tray and a pocket full of change.

"That's it!" said Laura triumphantly. "We're going to put you in business!"

Together they went to the local grocery store to buy more flour, sugar and oil. Sesi's coins were not enough to cover the cost of the ingredients, but Laura lent her the rest of the money. When they got home, Laura took out a pencil and paper and recorded the cost of the materials and the amount she had

212

lent Sesi.

Over the next few weeks they baked and sold doughnuts on different days of the week, recording their sales. It turned out that Tuesdays were the best days for the children, as they had tended to have the most pocket money that day.

"Tuesday it is," said Laura. "We'll go to the store on Mondays and get the ingredients, and then bake on Tuesday mornings. We'll also get you some bigger containers so you can carry more doughnuts."

The project was good for both women. Laura especially benefitted as it gave her something to focus her energy and attention on. But sometimes she would stop and look off into the distance, her features etched with sadness.

"He's in heaven with Figo. Figo is taking good care of him," Sesi said gently, folding her arms as if holding a baby.

Laura's eyes filled with tears. "I don't know how you can read my mind like that, Sesi, but thank you. That's so kind. I really like that image of your dear Figo holding my little baby Miguel, taking care of him."

"Where are you keeping the money from the sales?" asked Laura one afternoon after they finished counting their proceeds.

Sesi blushed and went to her bedroom. In a few minutes she returned and showed Laura an old coffee can where she stored the coins.

"That won't do," said Laura, shaking her head. "We need to open a bank account for you. Have you ever had one?"

"No."

"Okay, then let's go together."

The next morning, Laura went with Sesi to a bank.

"Will you vouch for her?" asked the kind clerk.

"Yes," said Laura and signed her name.

Sesi looked a bit green around the gills as she handed over her entire can of money in exchange for the savings book and Laura imagined for a moment that Sesi would cancel the transaction and run out of the bank. But instead, Sesi bit her lip and looked at Laura. Laura reassured her and they finished the process.

When they got home, Laura showed her how to keep track of the money on the little booklet that the bank had given her.

"We'll practice putting money in and taking money out," Laura said and saw the relief in Sesi's face.

As the weeks passed, sales continued going well, but the tuition for the school for Rocio was still out of reach.

"We have to expand the market," said Laura. "Let's take more walks and try to think of where else we can sell our doughnuts."

"The entrance to the university might be a good place. Maybe mid-morning?" said Sesi.

"Good idea," Laura agreed and soon they were making doughnuts to sell at two different locations, two different days a week. They charged the adults more and Sesi came home with her trays empty and a huge smile on her face.

Chapter 33

El Salvador, 1972

Sesi

Every day the newspapers published the disappearance of someone else. Most, if not all of the people who disappeared, were accused of being Communists. The logic was that Communists were terrible people and deserved to be killed. Being called a Communist by someone was a death sentence. I tried quietly to find out what a Communist was, but no one seemed to know. There were lots of poor people who were called Communists, but there were also middle class people who were accused of that. Priests and nuns who taught the villagers to boil water before feeding it to their babies were called Communists. Students like my dear Figo, and professors at universities were also accused of being Communists.

It was scary since you never knew who would be accused of it next. But it was a fear that you got used to living with. You kept your head down and did your work and hoped that no one would point a finger your way. Then one day it happens and your life is ruined. I didn't find out until after his death that Figo had been called a Communist, but I was on the lookout after that. I hoped I would never meet anyone else accused so unjustly. My hopes didn't come true.

More than two years after I had been working at *Doña*

215

Laura's house, after so many things had happened and my life was going so well and I had almost forgotten to be worried about the Communists, *Don* Adelmo got accused of being one and the events that occurred after that had a ripple on many of our lives.

I have perhaps neglected to tell you much about them before, so I ask your forgiveness. You have already seen that they were a very nice couple, both in their mid-thirties. They were kind, soft-spoken and respectful. *Don* Adelmo had worked as a professor for several years at the university, and before that he had been a high school teacher in the village of Atiquizaya, which was not terribly far from where I grew up. It was a very poor town, like most small villages, and he had been paid in chickens and tortillas because the government did not yet pay official wages for high school teachers.

Don Adelmo and his wife were dreamers, you see, and I'm now convinced that dreaming of a better future is one of the traits of Communists. *Don* Adelmo and *Doña* Adelgonda were not the very rich, nor were they the desolate poor, but rather, they were part of the slim slice of middle class. They were well off enough to have a *muchacha*, but that didn't take much. But they saw the disparity between the rich and the poor, something that many of us saw, and thought that it was not right.

That was not a typical thought, and it certainly was not a safe thought to vocalize anywhere where you could be overheard by the very rich. But, the sad thing is that dreamers go ahead and do things even if it puts them in danger, and that's what *Don* Adelmo did. He submitted articles to the newspaper which shone a light on inequalities, and, worst of all, he talked to his students at the university about his revolutionary ideas. That's what marks you as an especially bad Communist.

Early one morning, *Doña* Adelgonda's *muchacha* knocked at our door. When I saw her, I knew right away that it was bad news—it was kind of like when I had gone running to

216

their house, when *Doña* Laura lost her baby. When people came knocking at the door early in the morning, it could only be bad news.

The *muchacha* was visibly shaken and we couldn't get much out of her except that she thought that *Doña* Adelgonda needed help and could *Doña* Laura come immediately. It was a Wednesday morning, I remember, and *Don* Rodrigo Manuel had already gone to work and I had just returned from taking the children to school.

Doña Laura asked me to go with her, and I was glad to because I really didn't want her out there by herself and I did not stop to think, as I have since, that I would have been no more help to her than I ever was to Sara when I used to walk her to school, all those years ago.

When we got to *Doña* Adelgonda's house we saw her sitting on a chair in the kitchen, hunched over the green Formica table, sobbing disconsolately.

Doña Laura ran to her and put her arms around her, asking her what had happened and if there was anything that we could do to help. I'll never forget the intense grief on *Doña* Adelgonda's face when, after crying for an indeterminable time, she finally was able to speak to us.

"They found him," she said and began shuddering and sobbing again. "Oh, God help me, they found him and he's dead. Oh, dear God!"

I felt an intense pain in my chest when I heard that *Don* Adelmo had been killed. He was such a good man! I know because *Doña* Laura had invited me to join her on some evenings when *Doña* Adelgonda was over for a visit. I would sit quietly and crochet, as *Doña* Laura had taught me, while the men spoke in the kitchen and the children slept. So it was that I had sometimes unintentionally eavesdropped on their conversations and I knew that *Don* Adelmo was a decent human being.

217

Sometimes the men spoke of their classes at the university and of the students that were struggling. "Chema works in construction all day long," I heard *Don* Adelmo say, "and at night he goes home exhausted and tries to finish his math homework. I can see the bags under his eyes when he comes to class early in the morning, before he goes to his job. It's nearly impossible to work fifty hours a week and still do well in classes. But it's so frustrating because I can see his mind works well. If we could get some scholarships set up so people like him could afford not to work while they studied..."

Another time they were speaking of wages. "I agree with you, Adelmo," said *Don* Rodrigo, "I completely agree. When I lived in the U.S. there was a minimum wage which allowed people to survive. And if someone got sick or injured, they had the right to get that taken care of without losing their job..."

Just two weeks ago I heard them saying, "We need to find a way to make it a law that landowners can't abuse the poor people that live and farm on their land." I'm not sure which one of them it was because they were speaking in really low voices. If the door had not been left open, I would not have heard anything. But as it was, *Doña* Laura had gone into the kitchen to say her goodnight to her husband and then left without shutting the door. I stayed still in my spot, crocheting and thinking my own thoughts until I heard them practically whispering and that made me want to hear what they were saying.

I don't know why I have always been curious like this, but I meant no harm and did not ever speak of it. But based on what I remembered of Figo telling me, I'm pretty sure it was conversations like this one that got *Don* Adelmo into trouble with the *Escuadrones de la Muerte* who, everybody knew, were closely aligned with the very wealthy people.

"I knew something terrible had happened when he didn't come home last night," said *Doña* Adelgonda, hiccupping between sentences. Her face was wet and her nose was bright red. "I stayed up all night worrying, but there was nothing I could do. Then this morning there came a knock on the door. It was the police. They said he died when his car went over the edge of a narrow road, high on the volcano."

At this point poor *Doña* Adelgonda put her head down and cried and the other three of us ladies joined her. We cried because *Don* Adelmo was a good man and so young, the same age as *Don* Rodrigo Manuel, and it was a terrible shame to have him gone. We cried for a long time and looking back, I imagine that *Doña* Laura also cried because this death reminded her of losing poor *Don* Miguel and the wound in her heart was still fresh enough to bleed easily.

And for me, of course, the whole situation reminded me of what I went through when Alma had found Figo murdered. I had prayed fervently to the Virgin for years that no one would ever have to feel the pain that I had gone through, but She must not have been able to stop all the people who hate Communists because there were just too many. And when you hate Communists that bad, killing is nothing.

I don't think I exaggerate when I tell you that *Don* Adelmo's loss was a tremendous blow to humanity, even if most of humanity didn't know who he was. I think that's what happens whenever we lose a kind, good soul to senseless violence. Humanity becomes a bit poorer.

"They found him below the road, in the jungle, and they said you could see the path down the side of the mountain that the car made. They said that the whole car smelled like liquor and there was an almost empty bottle of whiskey on the floor of the passenger side."

But here's the thing, everyone knew that *Don* Adelmo was not a drinker. He never liked wine, let alone whiskey. He said it made him sick. So all of us immediately smelled a rat.

"There was no reason for him to be on that road, especially at that hour of the night, when he should have been home," she said. And it was true. That was a road you would only take if you were leaving town and *Don* Adelmo had no errands in that direction.

Doña Laura asked to use the phone to call *Don* Rodrigo Manuel, and he came right home. He was shaking so bad that he couldn't even fit the key to the lock to get in the door, and his face was streaked from where he had been crying. It made me want to cry fresh tears when I saw the devastation in his face.

That afternoon, he and *Doña* Laura went with *Doña* Adelgonda to see *Don* Adelmo at the morgue. But when they got a chance to see poor *Don* Adelmo, that's when they knew beyond any trace of a doubt that he had been murdered. Otherwise there's no way that the imprint of the butt of a rifle would have been so clearly visible on the side of his blood-splattered head.

Chapter 34

El Salvador, 1972

Sesi

After *Don* Adelmo was murdered, things around the country became even uglier. I thought they had been bad before, when my dear Figo was murdered, but it turned out that that was just the beginning and things were worse now. Anyone suspected of being a Communist was either threatened or outright killed. I quietly asked everyone I knew if they knew any Communists— this was not something you could talk about out loud for fear someone might hear you—but no one did. Still, someone must have been able to tell who they were and where they were hiding. Overnight, an image of a ghostly white hand, a *mano blanco*, would appear, spray-painted on the door to their house, or their car or their office, and that meant that that person was a Communist and they were now in the crosshairs of the *Escuadrones de la Muerte*.

It's really horrible how awful people can be to each other. It is beyond my feeble power to summon adequate words to describe to you the chaos and the anxiety that we lived during those dark years. I feared for us here in this most beautiful country of the whole world. I feared for all of humanity because the scriptures say that when our souls bleed hatred, it is the Savior, el Salvador, who cries. We joined Him in crying and we

221

are still crying now.

Everything changed after *Don* Adelmo's untimely death. For one thing, *Doña* Laura was very upset. In all the time I had known her, she was a woman who never seemed to raise her voice or get angry. Even after losing her poor little *Don* Miguel, she had been very sad and ill, though she was not angry. But in the weeks following *Don* Adelmo's death, she had several shouting matches with her husband. We could hear them, especially at night, hurling their words like grenades that the *guerrilleros* tossed from the jungle. Little Rodrigo and Isabella knew that something was wrong and they would come to my room and climb into bed with me and Rocio and we would crouch together, waiting for the storms to pass.

One morning, after a particularly acrimonious night, Laura told me that she no longer felt safe in this country. She wanted to move back to the United States, where people were not being tortured and beaten, their bodies dumped in the gutters or stuffed in cars and pushed down mountainous slopes. She said that in the United States there was not the disparity between the rich and the poor like there was here.

I lowered my eyes and turned away because I was ashamed that I lived in a country that could not keep a beautiful creature like *Doña* Laura safe and happy within its borders.

Don Rodrigo Manuel, not surprisingly, wanted to stay in El Salvador, the land where he had grown up and that he loved. Their fights were in English so I didn't understand the words, but it was not hard to get the idea. Also, *Doña* Laura could no longer speak with her close friend, *Doña* Adelgonda, since she had closed her house and moved away after the funeral. She went back to Sonsonate, where she had grown up, and now there was an even bigger void in our lives since we were missing both *Don* Adelmo and *Doña* Adelgonda. So, that is why *Doña* Laura

222

confided more in me.

She told me that *Don* Rodrigo Manuel had tried to convince her to stay by telling her that there had always been violence and that most of it was toward the poor. He told her that, in 1932, between 10,000 and 40,000 Pilpil Indians and rebels had been slaughtered because they were suspected of sympathizing with the communist revolutionary leader, Martí. It was just the way our country was with Communists.

What he meant was that since he and *Doña* Laura were not poor, if they just kept their heads down, nothing would happen to them.

Don Rodrigo Manuel also blamed the violence on the war that was going on with Honduras. There had been countless wars with this neighboring country. This latest one had begun recently, in 1969, after a soccer match. He was trying to say anything he could to keep her there, and I could understand that. Who would want to leave our beautiful country and go somewhere where they were treated poorly for something they could not control, like their skin color? And who would want to leave all the natural beauty of this country? I know I wouldn't have minded visiting other places, but even after everything that's happened, there is nothing that could have persuaded me to leave my beloved home country.

But after seeing *Don* Adelmo's bloodied skull that had been bludgeoned with the back of a rifle, *Doña* Laura could not be comforted. Two weeks after *Don* Adelmo's funeral, *Doña* Laura told me that she had given her husband an ultimatum. She and the children would be moving back to the United States the following week. He could either join her there or stay here.

"I told my Pop once that I would kill him if he ever touched me again," she said. "I know that I honestly believed that I would do it. I'm glad I never had to, but learning how to shoot a shotgun and knowing that I could do it, if I had to, gave me the strength to put my foot down when I need to. And I can feel it in my bones, Sesi, the way I felt it when I was fourteen years old, that this is what I need to do. I need to get out of this country with my children. I hope that my husband will choose to come with me. But if he doesn't, I'll find a way to make a life for us."

For a single mother to live alone with her children is a hardship. I knew that from personal experience and I couldn't imagine it would be an easier task anywhere else in the world. I also could not imagine ever leaving Figo, if that had been a possibility, which it wasn't. So, I just continued doing my chores, listening as she spoke.

"I've thought about it, and I realized that if I stay here and he gets killed, I will have no rights. I'm a foreigner and I look different and I talk different. I won't be able to sell the house or the car or anything. Everything is in his name. I wouldn't even be able to afford the airplane ticket back. Leaving now is the only thing I can do."

That was our last serious conversation. After that, the days slipped by like raindrops falling off the leaves of a tree, so quickly that you could not catch a single one of them.

In the end, *Doña* Laura got her way. She took the children and moved back to gringo-land. *Don* Rodrigo Manuel stayed behind for six weeks to sell the house and the furniture and the car. Then he went to join her. But, you should have seen him. He was like a ghost without her, walking around but not seeming to see anything. He hardly ate and he barely slept. I stayed on for two weeks, helping him clean things up and sell their belongings. *Doña* Laura took only what could fit in their suitcases because really, airplanes are not that big and you can't take everything with you when you fly on them.

Two weeks to the day after *Don* Rodrigo Manuel went to

224

the airport with two suitcases to meet with his wife and children in the land where things would be reversed and it would be he who looked strange and not speak the language as well, the military forces stormed the university with tanks. They lined up professors and students against the whitewashed walls where hot pink bougainvilleas flowered innocently. The soldiers tied the professors' hands with rough rope and covered their eyes with blindfolds and shot them dead before the afternoon rains came. Then they threw their limp bodies on trucks and hauled them off to pits wrestled from the jungle floor. Their families never even got to bury their remains.

So, it turns out that *Doña* Laura was right to insist on leaving the country or she surely would have been a widow by now. Or worse.

I sent her a letter telling her what happened and two months later, when I got a letter back from her, I could see that she had been crying as she wrote it because the paper had little wrinkle marks like it gets when drops of water spill on it and are dried.

Chapter 35

El Salvador, 1976

Sesi

As for me and Rocio, we have been two of the few fortunate people in my sad, troubled country. After *Doña* Laura left and I had helped *Don* Rodrigo Manuel clean up the house as much as possible, I went to live with *Doña* Flor Maria for a few months while I figured out what to do with my life. She was very kind and even allowed my little Rocio to stay with me at her house because I told her it was a temporary situation while I figured out what the next step would be.

Doña Laura, who was generous to me even as she was packing, left me some money and between that and what I had managed to save in the bank, I was able to take out a loan on a very small restaurant. It was her idea, as a matter of fact, that set the foundation for my survival after I no longer worked for her and the family. She started me out slowly, teaching me how to mix up the dough and cook the donus and then instructing me to go sell them at the doors of her children's school when I went to pick them up. Pretty much all of the kids had a little spending money and soon there were long lines of them waiting to snap up as many donus as I could make.

She loaned me money to buy the ingredients, then let me pay her back slowly from my profits. She taught me to keep track of my sales, and helped me to set up a bank account, something I had never dreamed of doing. She even gave me an afternoon off every week to buy supplies and take my donus farther away, to sell at parks or by the university. Then she encouraged me to save my money to be able to put Rocio in a better school. Without *Doña* Laura's friendship, guidance and direction, in all likelihood, I would have remained nothing more than a mediocre cook and a *muchacha* who liked to tell stories.

I opened my restaurant in Santa Tecla. Yes, you may smile at me since after striving all my life to get to San Salvador, I finally decided that being there was not what I wanted after all. Santa Tecla was where I had friends, and where my little Rocio could thrive. I also had *Doña* Flor Maria and *Don* Germán who were like family to me. They helped me to find the place that I bought. They even co-signed for the mortgage because I showed them my plan and the money that I had saved in my bank account.

The restaurant is just what I needed to finally be completely independent and not have to work as a *muchacha* at anyone's house anymore. It has a small kitchen and a few tables in front. In back there is a small room, where Rocio and I stay, and a bathroom. It is plenty for the two of us. I named it "Pastelería *Doña* Laura" in her honor and so that Rocio and I would never forget her generosity.

Right behind the building there is a huge mango tree and on many days we hear a large thonk on the roof. It always makes me smile because I know it is the sound of *Doña* Laura sending me good wishes in the form of mangoes dropping from the sky.

When I opened Pastelería *Doña* Laura, I immediately began making donus and selling them. People loved them and within eight months, I had more business than I could handle. So I sent word to Miranda, my old, dear friend with the scarred face, and she quit her job and joined me in the business. We aren't

227

rich, but we live comfortably and between her great cooking sense and what I learned from *Doña* Laura, we have managed to add several more items to the menu, though the donus are still the favorite thing for most of our customers.

I enrolled Rocio in the local school and continue to walk with her there every day to ensure that she can get an education. My dream is that one day she will be able to get into secretarial school and have a better life than me. I think she can do it because she is clever like her father and I now have enough money to pay for her education.

I wish I could tell you that life has been easy now that I am finally on my way to being financially independent. I wish I could say that the troubles that were brewing in El Salvador in the 1960s and early 1970s were resolved in an ethical and caring manner by intelligent people with big hearts. I wish I could say that good people who feel that the poor should be educated are no longer labeled as Communists and considered to be the enemy of the state.

I wish I could say that we no longer fear black Jeep Cherokees that pull up quietly in the night in front of someone's house and paint a white hand on the door.

But I can't tell you any of those things. My beautiful little country, filled with tall blue volcanoes and bounteous green jungles and miles of shimmering black-sanded beaches was sucked into a deep and hateful war that lasts even today. Too many innocent people have been slaughtered and too many aggressors, I fear, will never be brought to justice.

I can see how that could have made many of us bitter, wanting to tear out our hearts to let them shrivel and rot in the scorching, tropical sun. But mine is a beautiful country, with flowering maquilishuat trees and deep volcanic lakes of sweet, cool water. My countrymen are mostly honest, hard-working and lovely people. And while I am alive, I hope to always emulate

Doña Laura's spirit and never lose faith that one day we humans will come to our senses and dedicate ourselves to healing and nurturing with the enthusiasm that we have shown for war.

THE END

ACKNOWLEDGEMENTS

First I'd like to thank my mother for sharing stories from her stay in El Salvador. Although this book is in no way a biography, I was so young when we moved there that if I had to rely only on what I remembered, the narrative would have paled.

Thanks also to my cousin Paty who took the time to vet my questions and share stories from her childhood in ES. She was the first real friend of my life, from the time we were five years old, and I hold her dearly in my heart.

A big thank you to my cousin Greg for hosting us when we went for a visit to ES a few years ago. He spent a week running us around, feeding us and shuttling us from one interesting place to another. He was the first person to inspire/urge me to write a book about his beloved country. I hope you like this, Greg!

Another big shout out to my cousin Paco who was very generous when I asked him if he had any pictures I might use for the cover. He set up a huge album with hundreds of professional and stunning pictures and then sat with me for hours while I pored over them to find the perfect one. Thank you!

My friend Ruth Heeder was very helpful in her close attention to the manuscript, finding grammatical errors and cheering me on. Ruth, I appreciate your support.

My mother also deserves a hand for her careful reading of the manuscript and her encouragement.

Lauren Sapala, my editor and writing coach, deserves huge kudos for gently urging me on when I floundered and almost gave up entirely on writing this novel. She was a wonderful listener and guide and without her steady hand I'm sure this book would never have been born.

230

Finally, I'd like to thank my family for their unwavering support, especially my husband, who patiently read multiple drafts of this narrative, giving me sage advice. I couldn't do it without him!

CPSIA information can be obtained
at www.ICGtesting.com
Printed in the USA
LVOW13s2203201216

518186LV00007B/1372/P